THE GREAT IDEAS OF LILA FENWICK

Whether she's searching for the lost class pet, creating a prize-winning Halloween costume, or finding a quick but risky way to earn ten dollars, Lila Fenwick certainly can come up with Great Ideas.

With best friend Gayle and classmates Michael, Eddie, and Rita, Lila turns every problem into a hilarious and ingeniously solved adventure.

"The book captures both the funny moments and the touching aspects of preteen years...An outstanding choice..."
—ALA Booklist

THE GREAT IDEAS OF LILA FENWICK

Kate McMullan

pictures by Diane de Groat

Puffin Books

PUFFIN BOOKS
Published by the Penguin Group
Viking Penguin Inc., 40 West 23rd Street, New York, New York 10010, U.S.A.
Penguin Books Ltd, 27 Wrights Lane, London W8 5TZ England
Penguin Books Australia Ltd, Ringwood, Victoria, Australia
Penguin Books Canada Ltd, 2801 John Street, Markham, Ontario, Canada L3R 1B4
Penguin Books (N.Z.) Ltd, 182-190 Wairau Road, Auckland 10, New Zealand

Penguin Books Ltd, Registered Offices: Harmondsworth, Middlesex, England

First published in the United States of America by Dial Books for Young Readers, 1986
Published in Puffin Books, 1988
3 5 7 9 10 8 6 4
Text copyright © Kate McMullan, 1986
Illustrations copyright © Diane de Groat, 1986
All rights reserved
Printed in the United States of America
Set in Palatino

Library of Congress Cataloging in Publication Data
McMullan, Kate.   The great ideas of Lila Fenwick.
Summary: In a series of episodes, fifth grader Lila
Fenwick has some truly amazing "Great Ideas" that get
her out of and into all kinds of trouble.
[1. Schools—Fiction]   I. De Groat, Diane, ill.
II. Title. PZ7.M47879Gr   1988]
[Fic]   87-36028   ISBN 0-14-032499-2

for Jim

CONTENTS

THE GREAT IDEAS OF
LILA FENWICK

CHOCOLATE IS MISSING

Chocolate is missing.
He was last seen wearing a dark brown
fur coat and eating a carrot.
If you see him, contact
Lila Fenwick or Gayle Deckert,
in Mr. Sherman's room.
All information strictly confidential.

"What do you think?" I held the sign up for Gayle's approval.

"I think there's one tiny detail you forgot to mention," she said.

I read my sign over.

"You're right." I added: *Reward: $3.00.*

"You have to say what Chocolate is," Gayle said, "or people won't know what they're looking for."

Gayle had a point. She usually did. She could be as logical as a computer, as practical as notebook dividers. Sometimes I wondered how we ever got to be best friends. We not only thought differently, we looked about as unalike as two fifth graders could. Gayle is big, tall and wide, what you might call queen-sized. Her mother is always harping at her to lose ten pounds, but my mother says Gayle has "presence," which means she is very sure of herself and you notice her when she walks into a room. That's true, but even if Gayle weren't so large, you'd notice her because of her hair—wild, white-blond zig-zaggy hair.

My mother says I would have more presence if I'd trim my hair so that it didn't hang over my glasses and hide my "striking green eyes." But I've been trying to let my bangs grow out for six months, and I'd hate to give up and cut them now. I'm not sure it would help, anyway, because I'm short and bony and I have pretty ordinary brown hair. When I mention this, my mother says it's what's inside that counts.

I added one more line to the poster:

Chocolate answers to the description of a guinea pig.

Gayle sighed. "Too, *too* Nancy Drew."

Gayle had come over to my house after school to help make these posters about Chocolate. Making them had actually been my idea. I don't like to brag, but lots of times I get ideas. Not just good ideas, better than good—*great*. At school, where almost all the kids are known for something, I'm famous for my Great Ideas.

Of course all the kids in Mr. Sherman's room already knew that Chocolate was missing. He'd been our class pet. We'd gotten him on the first day of school, two weeks ago. I had suggested the name Chocolate for him and it had won in the class vote. (The other nominations were Squeaky, Fluffy, and George.) Everyone liked him a lot, and then, this morning, Tuesday morning to be exact, we'd come into the classroom and—no Chocolate. The door to his cage was standing open and he was gone.

Gone! Eddie English, our fifth grade Class President (who is known as T.K.O.—Total Knock-Out in the looks department), called a special meeting to discuss it.

"Does anybody know where Chocolate could be?" he asked, looking very serious.

"There's no way he got out of that cage by himself," volunteered Rita Morgan (also known as Miss Perfect), who had been in charge of changing Chocolate's cedar shavings on Monday. "I closed his cage up, like really tight, just before school let out yesterday." Rita paused dramatically and looked around the room. "I think," she announced, "that someone *stole* Chocolate."

I met Gayle at recess after the meeting. "What are we going to do?" I'd asked.

"About what?"

"Finding Chocolate. We've got to find him."

I had loved holding Chocolate in my lap, stroking his curly brown fur, scratching him behind the ears, and listening to him purr. When I thought that I might never hear that rattly purr again, I felt like crying.

Gayle just shrugged.

I tried to appeal to her interests. "But what if the person who took him doesn't know what to feed him? Doesn't know he likes apples and spinach leaves and peanut butter sandwiches? He could starve!"

"Guinea pigs'll eat anything," said Gayle. Where were her feelings?

What I needed right then was a Great Idea for making Gayle want to help me find Chocolate. With my imagination and Gayle's smarts, we'd be an unbeatable team. I went over to the jungle gym and hung by my knees, hoping that a flow of blood to my brain would stimulate my thinking. I could see Gayle, sitting right side up on the root of a big oak, reading *The Scarlet Band*. She loved to read Sherlock Holmes mysteries to see if she could figure out whodunit before Sherlock. Most of the time she could, since she has, as she modestly puts it, a mind like a steel trap. My face was almost scarlet before the Great Idea flowed into my brain.

I was beside Gayle in a nanosecond. Even if she didn't love Chocolate the way I did, I had a plan that would make her wild to find him.

"What we need to do," I'd announced, "is solve the Case of the Missing Chocolate."

Gayle glanced up from her book. "You mean conduct an investigation?"

"Precisely. Find clues, question suspects, the whole detective bit. Fenwick and Deckert, Private Eyes."

"Deckert and Fenwick? I like it." Gayle slammed her book for emphasis. "In three days," she predicted, "the guinea-grabber will be in our hands."

Now Gayle finished drawing one last pathetic picture of Chocolate underneath the notice I had written in black marker. She sat back on her heels and examined our lineup of posters.

"Not bad," she said.

I reached into my book bag and got out the SUR-PRISE! chocolate bars we'd bought to reward ourselves for doing all this work. I also took out my casebook. In it I'd kept a record of everything about the Case of the Missing Chocolate. That day during a health filmstrip I'd made a list of possible suspects. As we ate our candy bars I showed it to Gayle.

Who Took Chocolate?

Possible Suspects / Possible Motives:

1. Rita Morgan
Today I saw Rita's mother's station wagon parked at school and in the back was a

> shopping bag with three heads of lettuce on top. Guinea pigs eat tons of lettuce.
>
> 2. Sandra Guth
> Sandra has a snake. I read once that snakes sometimes need to have a live meal. Maybe Sandra took Chocolate to use for snake food.
>
> 3. Michael Watson
> As everyone knows, Michael is a science genius. As everyone also knows, guinea pigs are often used in science experiments. Michael may have taken Chocolate to use in some awful experiment.

A look of amazement came over Gayle's face as she read my list.

"Sandra's snake," she began, "it's a garter snake. It eats teensy frogs. And Sandra is hardly the type to steal the class pet."

Gayle was right. Sandra was the most popular kid in our class. Besides, Sandra's mom let her have a snake, didn't she? If Sandra wanted a guinea pig, her mom would probably let her get one. She wouldn't have to steal.

"So scratch her off the list."

"As for Rita," Gayle went on, "I overheard her at lunch today saying that her mother has the whole family on another disgusting diet, and for supper they

YOU ARE HERE

MISSING

"CHOCOLATE"

ANSWERS TO THE
DESCRIPTION OF A
GUINEA PIG Conrad von
Room 302

can only eat tossed salads with lemon juice and anchovies."

"Gross." That explained the lettuce. "You'd better hope Rita's mother doesn't tell your mother about this diet."

Gayle ignored my comment. "Plus, what would Rita want with a guinea pig anyway? You do remember her whining about getting stuck with the job of changing the cage yesterday, don't you? She said she'd need a new manicure if she had to touch 'the rodent.'"

It was all coming back to me now. "I guess we can take her off the list, too."

"That leaves Michael," said Gayle. "You really think your old buddy Michael would take Chocolate to experiment on?"

"He might," I told her. I'd known Michael practically forever. I could remember baby Michael trying to say Lila, but coming out with YiYa. I think that's why, to this day, he calls me Fenwick. But friend or not, he was still a suspect. "Michael *is* a total science weirdo. He might have stolen Chocolate and not even feel bad about it if he was working on some terribly important project." My imagination clicked into high gear. "Like curing leprosy or . . . or . . . communicating with aliens."

"Leprosy?" Gayle raised her eyebrows. "Aliens? With a guinea pig?"

"Well, curing the common cold, maybe." I wasn't giving up on Michael. "I remember hearing Chocolate sneeze a few times. Maybe Michael just borrowed Chocolate and he's planning to bring him back—if he survives the experiment."

"Borrowed." Gayle looked thoughtful. "It's possible, I guess." She gave me a Sherlockian stare. "Let's interrogate him tomorrow at lunch."

"Hi, Michael," I said as Gayle and I slid our trays next to his at the long, blond cafeteria table where he had been sitting by himself. Michael always ate lunch alone. Today he was reading a book called *Giant Ants of the Third Galaxy* while he ate.

Michael looked up over his book and smiled. "Greetings, earthlings."

Gayle wasn't into beating around the bush. "Say, Michael," she began, "been conducting any experiments lately? You know, any science experiments?"

Michael looked at Gayle strangely.

I tried to help. "Biology experiments maybe?"

"What's the sudden interest in biology?" Michael asked. He took a large bite of his Sloppy Joe. Michael was one of the few kids who bought a plate lunch every day and actually ate it.

"Uh . . . I'm thinking of taking a Saturday class," I began. "At the Museum of Natural History in . . . uh . . ."

Gayle tried to save me. "In animal experiments."

"That's right," I said.

Michael popped a rubbery orange jello cube into his mouth. Our interrogation was getting nowhere.

"You know," I piped up, "like, maybe, a class in cat dissection."

Michael's eyes widened. "You want to spend your Saturday mornings cutting up dead cats? Boy, Fenwick, you're even weirder than I thought you were."

That's when I remembered Michael's beloved cat, Nelson.

Gayle decided to catch our suspect off guard with the direct approach. "Michael, did you borrow Chocolate to experiment on?"

Michael stared in disbelief first at Gayle and then at me. "You think I've stolen Chocolate and dissected him, is that it?" He looked down at his plate for a few seconds, then he slowly raised his eyes to meet mine. "The truth is, it's even worse than that," he said.

"Worse?" I almost shouted. "What could be worse than being dissected?"

Michael picked up his Sloppy Joe and slowly pried off the top bun. "I'm eating him for lunch!" Michael started laughing like a maniac. "Chocolate on a bun!" He shoved his Sloppy Joe in my face. "Try some!"

"Michael," I said sternly. "This is serious."

But my partner in investigation was cracking up, while I sat there and worried. Now we didn't have one single suspect left on our list.

I always walk home from school alone on Wednesdays because Gayle has her ballet lesson on that day. On this particular Wednesday I walked slowly. I wanted time to think. I also wanted time to enjoy the SURPRISE! chocolate bar that I'd been saving all day. Maybe it would help me solve the Case of the Missing Chocolate. I peeled the wrapper down. The chocolate coating on the candy bar was just the color of Chocolate's fur. It made me feel sad and hungry at the same time. Who could have stolen Chocolate? Who would be creepy enough to take a class pet? I pulled the candy bar all the way out of the wrapper, reading the label as I walked. *A candy bar that's full of surprises!* it said. *A chocolate escape from the ordinary.* A chocolate escape. And then it hit me like a ten-pound box of bonbons—maybe Chocolate hadn't been stolen at all! He might have escaped! Rita could have thrown us all off the track by claiming to have closed the cage tightly. Snapping that cage door shut wasn't easy. No doubt Rita was afraid if she did it, she'd break a nail. She probably left the cage door wide open but didn't want to get blamed for Chocolate getting out, so she invented the stealing angle. It suddenly seemed so clear to me. Maybe Chocolate was somewhere in the classroom, huddled in a corner, scared, hungry, and miserable!

I stuffed the remains of the SURPRISE! into my mouth, turned around, and ran back to school. I called my mom from the office and she agreed to pick me up in half an hour if I'd help her put together her new Body-Toner Rowing Machine when I got home.

Then I raced all over the building until I found Mr.

Todd, the maintenance man. I tried to explain what I was doing and asked him to let me into the classroom so I could look for Chocolate.

He sounded skeptical at first. "You say there's a pig loose in your classroom?"

"A guinea pig!" I shouted. I held my hand about six inches apart to show him the size.

"A mini-pig?" He shook his head. "Never heard of a pig that small." He shook his head all the way to Mr. Sherman's room, but he let me in, saying he'd be back in about ten minutes.

I flipped on the lights and poked around the room for a while, without results, until I remembered a story I'd read once about this wizard. He could find anything by pretending to *be the thing*. I would *be the thing*!

"I am a guinea pig. I am a guinea pig," I told myself as I got down on my hands and knees beside Chocolate's cage and crawled away from it, wriggling my nose and squeaking just like a real guinea pig would do. I stuck close to the brown wooden baseboards all the way along one wall. I rounded the corner and was so into *being the thing* that I never noticed Roger Rupp's ruler sticking out of the side of his desk until it caught me—*thwack!*—right above the eyebrows. I straightened up fast, bashing the back of my head into the plywood board holding Kelly MacConnell's salt and flour map of Brazil and sending my glasses flying. Deciding that it was too painful to *be the thing*, I sat down, knocking the metal grate off a heating vent with my knee as I did so. It's a good thing I get Great Ideas, I thought. Otherwise I'd definitely be known as Class Klutz.

I found my specs under Barney Barker's desk, put them on, and then carefully bent down to peer into the dark rectangular hole of the vent. I couldn't see a thing. I was just getting up my nerve to stick my arm into the vent to feel around for Chocolate, when suddenly I sensed that I wasn't alone. Turning my head, I saw a pair of perfectly scuffed sneakers behind me. Slowly I looked up past the sneakers, past the khaki pants, past the plaid shirt, and into the T.K.O. gorgeous face of Eddie English. There he was, wearing his Fifth Grade Safety Patrol Badge, just standing, watching me. From where I was, I noticed, I could see right up his nose.

"Why'd you sneak up on me?" was all I could think to ask.

"Why'd you sneak in here after hours to crawl around?"

"I didn't just sneak in here to crawl around," I explained, wondering whether he had been standing there to see me sniffing, guinea pig–style, along the floor. "On the way home today I happened to think that Chocolate might not have been stolen at all. He might have escaped from his cage and be hiding somewhere in this room, so I came back to have a look."

Eddie sat down by me. "Sounds reasonable," he

said. I noticed then that his eyes were dark, dark brown, the color of the bittersweet chocolate my mom uses for making chocolate cakes.

Without my even hinting, Eddie shoved his arm into the furnace vent, all the way up to his shoulder.

"I can't feel anything," he said, "but this goes clear to the furnace. Maybe we should ask Mr. Todd to let us look down there."

"I already thought of that," I said quickly. I mean, Eddie English may be cute, but this was my case, after all. "Lucky thing the furnace hasn't been turned on yet this year."

Just then Mr. Todd poked his head in the door. "Sooey! Sooey!" He laughed. "That's how we used to call the pigs on the farm when I was a boy. Any sign of your pig yet?"

"Guinea pig!" I yelled again. "No, not so far."

Then I showed him the heating vent cover and explained how I'd knocked it off.

Mr. Todd nodded. "It's always falling off. Haven't had time to fix it yet."

That was bad news for Chocolate. Could he have crawled down the vent? As best I could, I shouted to Mr. Todd what I thought might have happened to the poor guinea pig, and he agreed to check the furnace room carefully.

As he let us out of the classroom, Mr. Todd winked. "A pig in the furnace room. I never saw such a thing! Get it? Pig? Never *sausage* a thing?" He chuckled.

I looked at Eddie. He just rolled his chocolate-cake eyes at me. Some joke.

"Well, Lila," my dad said that night as we finished eating supper, "any luck with the Case of the Restless Cavy?"

I shook my head. Was I the only one who didn't think Chocolate's disappearance was something to joke about? When my class got Chocolate at school, I brought home a library book about guinea pigs and my dad and I read it together. Their scientific name really is Restless Cavy. We also found that Chocolate is what's known as a Brazil guinea pig because of his curly hair.

My dad went into the kitchen and came back carrying a tray with three big bowls of what looked like chocolate ice cream drowning in chocolate syrup. We almost always have fresh fruit for dessert, so I could hardly believe my eyes.

My dad gave me a little squeeze. "This is to bring you luck in your search for Chocolate," he said.

"This is *real* chocolate ice cream?" I asked. "Not some phony carob look-alike?"

"It's the genuine article," my mom answered.

"Fifteen extra minutes on the Body-Toner for you tomorrow, Mom," I told her.

"Well worth it," she declared, digging out a huge spoonful of chocolate-smothered ice cream and holding it up as if she were making a toast. My dad and I raised our dripping spoons together to meet hers.

"Here's to you, Chocolate," my mom said. "Wherever you may be."

After helping with the dishes, I went up to my room. I had a funny feeling there was something I was supposed to do. Then I saw my casebook lying on the bed, and I remembered that I'd promised myself to write in it every night until the Chocolate Case was closed. But tonight, I figured, why bother. All I would have written anyway was: *It seems like Lila Fenwick has run out of Great Ideas.*

The next morning our class began as usual with a meeting. This was Mr. Sherman's way of letting us get used to being more grown up and deciding some things for ourselves. So far Sherman Tank, as we had nicknamed him because he was so big, was turning out to be okay. He was fair, he could be both funny and serious, and he treated us as if he just assumed we'd do our best work—even Barney Barker, Class Airhead.

Eddie English and his Oreo eyes were running the meeting, so it was hard not to pay attention, but I was still trying desperately to think of new ways to look for Chocolate. When no one had anything to report about our missing pet, we went on to the next topic on the agenda: the class field trip to the Museum of Natural History. I could feel Michael Watson's eyes on the back of my neck the whole time we were discussing the trip!

When the meeting was over, Mr. Sherman stood up.

"Well," he said, "today is Thursday, September twenty-fifth. I've been looking forward to this date because I am eager to hear your oral reports on South America which are due today."

Desks squeaked open and report folders began appearing in front of everyone. My heart started pounding. Reports! I'd totally forgotten about these reports! Mr. Sherman would think I was the Class Airhead instead of Barney Barker. My report was on the main products of Brazil. Let's see, what had I read that day at the library? There was coffee. I remembered that. And cattle. Sugar. What else?

I saw Gayle waving her hand, hoping Mr. Sherman would let her begin the reports. Oral reports were Gayle's specialty. She got to show how smart she was and ham it up at the same time. Please, Mr. Sherman, I thought, pick Gayle.

"Why don't we start somewhere in the middle of the alphabet today?" Mr. Sherman said, looking down at his class list. "Let's see. I turn my desk over to Lila Fenwick."

Why me? I thought. What have I done to deserve this? My heart was bonging so loud! It sounded like a stick pounding on a garbage can lid. I didn't even know if I'd be able to walk, but somehow I got to the front of the room, after tripping just a little over Barney Barker's fat foot, which he stuck out on purpose. I stood behind the little podium on Mr. Sherman's desk.

"No notes?" Mr. Sherman asked.

"No, sir," I said. "I guess it's all in my head."

"Excellent." Mr. Sherman smiled. "Go ahead then."

"My report is on the main products of Brazil," I began. "The biggest product of Brazil is coffee, which comes from the coffee bean. Coffee beans grow on low trees. The fact that the trees aren't very tall makes it easy for coffee bean pickers to pick the coffee beans."

I looked around me. I could see that everyone in the whole class was bored already. Rita was writing a note with a pink pen that had a plastic unicorn on top. Even though she was way back in the fifth row, I could smell the strawberry scent of her ink.

"Coffee is a popular drink all over the world, so Brazil exports tons of it each year."

Even Gayle was doodling on her notebook cover. And then, as I talked, I noticed Rita passing her note to Eddie English. Well, there was no way I was going to stand up in front of everyone going on and on about exports and main products while Eddie English read a note from a girl who wrote with phony strawberry ink—a girl who lived on lettuce and little salty fish—a girl who didn't care one little bit that Chocolate was missing! Even if I don't have a lot of information, I thought, I'm going to make Eddie English listen to me. Luckily, at that very moment, I was struck by a Great Idea.

"It might surprise you to learn that something which we all know and love would be missing from our diets if it weren't for the main products of Brazil."

Everyone looked wide awake now.

I kept on. "That's right. First of all, there are lots of cows in Brazil. And as everyone knows, cows give milk. There's also plenty of sugarcane growing there, so sugar is a main product. And then my personal favorite: There are lots of cocoa plants, which produce cocoa beans, which are ground up to make— chocolate. So, if you mix chocolate and sugar and milk together, you get what we all know as a milk chocolate candy bar!"

Everyone in the class, including Eddie English, laughed—even Lynn Williamson, who was incredibly shy and hardly ever even smiled. Then I realized that they were all waiting for me to go on. But my mind was blank. I couldn't remember one more fact about the products of Brazil. I thought about concluding my report by eating a candy bar. I twisted the hair of my bangs. Think, I told myself. Think! My knees were trembling. I tried to stop them by straightening my legs and tucking the toes of my sneakers under Mr. Sherman's bottom desk drawer, which was open a crack. But as I did this, the toe of one sneaker caught under the drawer, and when I tried to pull it out, the drawer slid open and knocked my other foot out from under me. I lost my balance and fell, hard, right on my behind.

"Chocolate is only one product of a big country like Brazil," I spoke out above the giggles, as I pulled myself back to a standing position on Mr. Sherman's desk. I kept talking, about rubber trees I think, but my mind was on that drawer. I'd seen something dark inside, dark and furry. Careful not to get my foot stuck again, I opened the drawer the rest of the way and there, curled up in a little nest of shredded paper, was the missing Chocolate. Not only that, but nestled beside Chocolate were three little guinea pigs no bigger than after-dinner mints.

"And that concludes my report," I said. One look at Mr. Sherman's face told me that he didn't think it had been such a fantastic report, but I went on quickly. "I have something else to report. Another kind of chocolate from Brazil—our guinea pig Chocolate—has been found. And he, I mean *she*, has three babies!"

So many things happened at once then. The whole class filed quietly by the desk drawer to take a peek at mother Chocolate and her brood. Then everyone got an extra recess while Mr. Sherman and Gayle and I fixed up Chocolate's cage. We put in a big tent-shaped piece of cardboard so that the guinea pigs could have some privacy. We gave them water and lots of food and put the cage in a semi-quiet part of the classroom.

Of course we held another name contest for the babies and ended up with Chocolate Sundae, Chocolate Kiss, and . . . George, which was Barney Barker's idea of a joke.

Later Mr. Sherman called me up to his desk. He said he found my report a bit short on hard facts, but that considering the circumstances which interrupted me, I could turn in a written report later in the week. He also congratulated me on solving the Case of the Missing Chocolate and said that if I'm really a great detective, in a couple of months I'll be able to find good homes for the babies. I've already started working on a list of possible suspects.

THE
SPIDER'S WEB

Gayle Deckert, my best friend since second grade, hadn't said a word to me all week. Her last words had been: "Lila, I'll never forgive you for this."

It all started one morning when Gayle and I were walking to school and I told her that my mom had said I couldn't go trick-or-treating on Halloween.

"You're kidding," said Gayle. "That's horrible. "Why not?"

"Remember last year," I asked, "when that guy across town was arrested for putting poison in some Halloween cupcakes and six or seven kids ended up in the hospital emergency room? Well, my mom saw something about it in the paper this morning and she said no trick-or-treating. Period."

As we reached the front steps of Price School, Gayle gave me a look so full of pity that it made me want to cry. Halloween was her favorite holiday, and no wonder. It had all the elements she loved: a chance to wear a great costume, a chance to parade around acting out a part, and best of all, a chance to fill a pillowcase with candy corn, little marzipan pumpkins, red licorice whips, black licorice cats, miniature Baby Ruths, Butterfingers, Heath Bars, Milky Ways, Snickers, and juicy red wax lips. If anyone could understand why I was upset, it was Gayle.

"You're still going to go, though, right?" I asked Gayle as we walked into school. "Trick-or-treating, I mean."

Gayle looked at me. "I hate to tell you this, Lila," she said, "but I wouldn't miss it for the world."

"The class meeting will now come to order," said Eddie English, speaking comfortably in the formal language of Roberts Rules of Order, which Mr. Sherman insisted that we use to "conduct class business efficiently." Eddie perched on a corner of Mr. Sherman's desk, looking like a natural executive. I had no trouble imagining that someday he'd be conducting meetings in the Oval Office. "Any old business?"

Kelly MacConnell reported on the project to buy a school flag. Barney Barker asked if anyone had seen his blue windbreaker, because if he didn't find it soon, his mother was going to take the price of a new one out of his allowance. No one had seen it.

"Any new business?" asked Eddie.

Rita Morgan's pink polished hand flew up. She came to the front of the room to stand next to Eddie to make her announcement.

"My uncle," she began, "has this vegetable farm about fifty miles from here."

What this had to do with class business, I didn't know.

"And," Rita went on, blinking at Eddie, "he used this new fertilizer this year and grew this totally dynamite pumpkin that weighs almost two hundred pounds. And he said that, if we want, he'll bring it over in his pickup truck and we can make it into a jack-o'-lantern."

"The jack-o'-lantern that ate Milwaukee!" bellowed Barney Barker, never one to let Roberts Rules of Order stand in the way of what he had to say. Everyone started talking at once then. I had to admit it sounded pretty neat, a two-hundred pound pumpkin.

"All in favor?" asked Eddie.

Everybody's hand went up. Barney Barker held up two hands so he'd get counted twice. The motion carried. And, suddenly, thinking about such a huge jack-o'-lantern and how weird and spooky it would look at night, I was possessed by a Great Idea.

"Any other new business?" asked Eddie. He saw my hand. "Lila?"

I stood up. "I've been thinking about Halloween,

and the fact is, we're getting a little bit old for trick-or-treating." I tried hard not to look at Gayle. "So, now that we're going to have a big jack-o'-lantern, maybe we should have a big class party, too, on Halloween night, you know, with a spook house and . . . ,"—I'd saved the best till last—"prizes for the best costumes."

"You mean skip trick-or-treating?" Roger Rupp sounded worried. "But what about all the candy and stuff?"

"My mom makes me dump most of mine out anyway," admitted Sandra Guth.

"Mine, too," echoed Kelly MacConnell.

"Then let's have the party!" shouted Barney Barker. "I'm coming as a Hercules Horrorshow, the wrestler!"

"I'm coming as a rock star!" yelled Sandra.

"I'm gonna be a robot!" called out Tim Petefish.

"What are you coming as, Rita?" hooted Barney Barker. "A witch?"

"She can't be a witch!" shouted Tim. "She has to wear a costume, remember?"

"Very funny." Rita poked the tip of her tongue out at Tim. "I'm coming as a movie star," she announced.

Everyone seemed so excited about the idea of the party, I was sure that my mother wasn't the only one who'd said "absolutely no" to trick-or-treating.

"All in favor of having the party at school, raise your hand," said Eddie.

"Wait," broke in Mr. Sherman. "I've just remembered. I'm afraid it's against administration policy to have parties on school grounds after school hours."

"But what about the sixth grade luau last year?" asked Kelly MacConnell. "That was a party, and it was at night."

"True," said Mr. Sherman. "But that luau was the culmination of the class study of Hawaii."

We all must have looked pretty disappointed then, because Mr. Sherman started tapping the eraser of his pencil on his chin, which is a sign that he's thinking.

"I've got it!" he said after a minute. "We could have the Halloween party as a language arts enrichment activity if you'd all agree to come costumed as your favorite book characters."

No one said anything. Now it was Mr. Sherman's turn to look disappointed. He stood up. "I can tell you think I'm trying to turn Halloween into a giant book report, which, I assure you, is not the case."

"Do you mean we're supposed to come dressed as Winnie the Pooh or something?" asked Kelly MacConnell.

"You *could* come as Winnie the Pooh," said Mr. Sherman, "or Alice in Wonderland or Captain Hook or Frankenstein's Monster or Dracula or Mr. Hyde."

"But aren't those guys from the movies, Mr. Sherman?" asked Barney Barker.

"They're in movies now," said Mr. Sherman, "but they were in books first."

"Do we have to read the book?" Barney asked.

Mr. Sherman looked like he was trying not to lose his patience. "It would be helpful to get the book as research so you'd know something about the character."

By now everyone was whispering and getting into the idea.

"All in favor of having a class party on Halloween night where we come dressed as book characters, raise your hand." Eddie counted twenty-six hands.

"All opposed?"

Two hands went up. One belonged to Barney Barker, who was probably still afraid he might have to read a book. The other hand belonged to Gayle.

"The yes votes have it," declared Eddie. "The meeting is adjourned."

And that's when, as we were getting ready for Social Studies, Gayle came up to me and said in a low voice, "Lila, I'll never forgive you for this."

I knew that Gayle meant what she said. After school I belly flopped onto my bed to think things over. On the one hand I was glad that I'd been able to turn what could have been a truly dismal Halloween for me into a party. On the other hand I felt bad that I'd turned what could have been a truly glorious Halloween for Gayle into a school function. For me, the party, however book-reportish it might turn out to be, was better than nothing. But for Gayle, no matter how wonderful the party was, it could never hold a candle to good, old-fashioned trick-or-treating. Deep down inside I thought that Gayle had every right to be furious with me.

To make myself feel better I started thinking about my costume. I wanted to be Charlotte, the spider from *Charlotte's Web*, and I already had a Great Idea for a costume. I'd wear dark gray tights, a long, dark gray sweat shirt, and a black ski mask, the kind with only eye, nose, and mouth holes. Then I'd sew yarn all around my costume so that I'd look like I was in the middle of a web!

I thought that my spider costume idea was even greater than most of my Great Ideas, and I felt like I just *had* to win one of the prizes. Sandra Guth always won all the sports prizes. Gayle got all the prizes at the end of each year for Outstanding Achievement in Math, Social Studies, Language Arts—anything that required brainpower. Kelly MacConnell took all the prizes in the Art Fair every year, and of course, Michael always walked away with the Science Fair blue ribbons. Winning the prize for the best Halloween costume would take lots of imagination, and imagination was my specialty. How would it feel, I wondered, to step up to the judges, the way I'd seen Gayle and Michael do so many times, and be handed a prize? Here was *my* chance to find out.

I closed my eyes and pictured myself as Charlotte inside her web. I'd always loved Charlotte. She was one talented spinner. When her friend Wilbur the pig learned that he was being fattened up to become smoked bacon and ham, Charlotte spun words into her web, spelling out just what a remarkable pig Wilbur was. Talk about Great Ideas! In the middle of her web, she wrote: SOME PIG! And those words saved Wilbur's life. Charlotte was the best friend Wilbur could have had.

Thinking about best friends made me think about Gayle again. I crossed my fingers and made a wish that before long I'd have my best friend back.

The next morning, during the class meeting, Mr. Sherman put five pieces of paper up on the bulletin board.

"These are the Party Committee sign-up sheets," he explained. "Now, we'll need a Decorations Committee, a Refreshment Committee, an Entertainment Committee, a Costume Prize Committee, and a Clean-Up Committee. There is a number at the top of every sheet that tells how many members each committee will need. Sometime today or tomorrow take a moment to sign up for the one you would like to work on."

"Any other new business?" asked Eddie English. There was silence. "Meeting's adjourned."

With that, every single kid in our class made a mad dash for the sign-up sheets. Luckily I sit very close to the bulletin board. I had my newly sharpened pencil in my hand, and I was the first one to the Entertainment Committee sign-up sheet. But unluckily, when I pressed my pencil to the paper ,the point snapped. By the time I ran back to my desk to get another pencil, all that was left to sign up for was, you guessed it, the Clean-Up Committee.

Later that day the class broke into committee groups to make plans. Michael Watson, who had been at a dental appointment during the sign-up crunch, was the other Clean-Up Committee member.

"Well, Fenwick," he said, "got any Great Ideas about how we're going to clean up after the party?"

"With some *big* trash bags," I said.

That was about all the planning our committee needed.

"What book character are you coming as?" I asked Michael.

"It's supposed to be a secret," he reminded me.

We spent the rest of our committee planning time reading. I noticed that Michael was reading a book called *The Green Thing from the Planet Orkon*. Big secret, I thought.

The rest of that week we did hardly any schoolwork. The Decorations Committee carved the jack-o'-lantern. The face had a wide, jagged mouth and pop eyes made by sticking gourds into the eye sockets. The Entertainment Committee was planning a gigantic spook house. The rumor from the Refreshment Committee was that parents were insisting on "wholesome treats." I hoped their kids could talk them into some "not-so-wholesome treats," too. The Prize Committee had asked our principal, Ms. Alexander, and our art teacher, Ms. Sherry, to judge the costumes. No one was to tell who they were supposed to be. We were to memorize a clue from the book to help people guess. But the best news of all was from Barney Barker on the Costume Prize Committee. His family owned a movie theater, and—since he had found his blue windbreaker the night before—his mother had agreed to give free movie passes for a whole year to the winners of the Best Person and Best Animal book characters!

Thinking about winning such a great prize was the only thing that made me feel good at all in the days that followed. Gayle still wouldn't talk to me. She ate lunch by herself every day. I tried having lunch with Sandra and Kelly, but they spent most of the time giggling, and I wasn't in a laughing mood. I sat with Michael once, and he explained to me in great detail the amazing fall migration path of the yellow warbler. I missed my best friend so much I could hardly stand it.

On the day of Halloween Gayle was still giving me the silent treatment. I'd tried and tried to think of a Great Idea for making up with her, but my mind seemed full of cobwebs.

Since I couldn't make my costume with Gayle, I decided to see if my mom would help. I found her, as usual, in the basement, rowing away on her Body-Toner.

"How would you like to help me finish making my Halloween costume?" I asked her.

"Ten . . . more . . . minutes," she panted.

I headed up to my bedroom and pulled on my tights and my dad's hooded sweat shirt, which hit me at the knees. When my mom finally puffed up the stairs, I showed her how I'd already started sewing pieces of yarn connecting the arms of the sweat shirt with the outsides of my tights. Then I stood with my legs stretched apart and my arms over my head while my mom finished sewing on my web—what seemed like hundreds of pieces of silvery yarn.

At last my mom said, "There. Done." She bit the thread she'd been sewing with.

I whipped off my glasses and pulled on my ski mask, lifting the sweat shirt hood over it. I walked stiffly to the full-length mirror. I squinted. Did I look like a spider in the middle of a web or more like I'd lost a fight with a shawl? I slipped my glasses back on to take a better look. I'd been afraid they'd spoil my costume, but instead they gave me a nice spidey-eyed look.

"Put your feet farther apart, Lila, and your arms up higher," directed my mom. "There. That's better."

I *did* look arachnidlike when I stood that way. My costume was, to borrow one of Charlotte's words, TERRIFIC!

"But I'm not sure I can do this for two hours at the Halloween party," I confessed.

"You won't need to," my mom said. "You only have to look perfect for the judging."

I stuffed my ski mask into the sweat shirt pocket

and checked the mirror again. No one could have a more original animal costume, I thought. Impossible.

"Thanks, Mom," I said. "I wish you could be there to see me win the prize!" I planted two big kisses on her cheek.

"Ummm! Spider kisses!" she exclaimed, giving me a squeeze before she headed downstairs. "I'll be ready to drop you at school in five minutes."

Racing to brush my teeth, I somehow managed to trip over a door stopper, and as I toppled, I banged my knees on the hard tile floor. Slowly I got up, shaking out my legs and thinking that it was a good thing I wasn't a real spider. Imagine having bruised knees on *eight* legs!

Then I noticed that a couple of pieces of yarn had pulled out from my heel. Quickly I sewed them back on, thinking that it was lucky this had happened here at home where I could fix it. "Be prepared!" my ex-Boy Scout father is always telling me, so I slipped a needle and thread into my sweat shirt pocket just in case I started coming unwebbed again.

My mom drove me to school and let me off in front.

"I'll be back to pick you up at nine o'clock," she said.

"Better make it nine thirty," I told her. "I'm on the Clean-Up Committee, remember?"

I walked up the sidewalk behind a Pippi Long-stocking and a Laura from the *Little House* books. Right beside me was someone dressed all in brown, with a pointy nose and a few wispy black whiskers.

"Are you a rat from *Mrs. Frisby and the Rats of NIMH*?" I guessed.

"No!" came a muffled voice from behind a mask. "I'm supposed to be a dog!"

So far, so good, I thought. This dog was no competition for the Best Animal Costume prize.

Our room looked just great! It was pretty dark and the jack-o'-lantern shone eerily, even though it did have to be lit with flashlights to meet the school fire code. Everywhere there were Day-Glo skeletons and bats dangling on thin strings.

I went farther into the room and spotted Gayle. She was wearing a hat with woolly earflaps that I'd often seen her father put on when he took out the garbage on a chilly evening. She had on his big checkered wool coat, too, which almost dragged on the floor. Her teeth were clenched around a pipe. Who was she supposed to be? Sherlock Holmes? I couldn't exactly tell. But one thing was for sure. Gayle wasn't going out for any prizes tonight. She hadn't even bothered to tuck her zigzag hair up under her cap so she'd look like ol' Sherlock. And then I noticed the oddest thing: Under her big coat I saw the cuffs of her yellow flannel pajamas. Pajamas! I was dying to ask her what that was all about, but she still had such a pouty face, I just looked away.

Lots of people were waiting to go into the spook house, and I got in line, too. Beside the line there were about a hundred marshmallows hanging from strings just above our heads. While we waited in line, we were supposed to hold our hands behind our backs and try to pull off the marshmallows with our teeth. I tried for a couple, but then I saw Barney Barker going down the row of marshmallows and licking them all, so I decided to quit.

At the entrance to the spook house, there was Eddie. He wasn't dressed as anything as obvious as Dracula—but Tim Petefish and Roger Rupp both were. His costume was perfect: a knight in shining armor. He looked so handsome, even though, up close, you could tell his armor was made from aluminum foil. Those big brown eyes of his peering out from under his helmet made me wish I'd come to the party as a fancy lady instead of a bug.

"Step right up!" called Eddie. "Come to the Dead Body Spook House!"

I stepped in. It was totally dark. Suddenly a hand took my hand and shoved it into a bowl of something cold and clammy.

"These are the brains of the Dead Body," said a voice that sounded very much like Tim Petefish.

"Gross," I said. "Leftover spaghetti."

"And," the voice continued, "here is the heart of the Dead Body."

He put my hand on something else, even more slimy.

"What is this?" I whispered. "Chicken livers?"

"It was supposed to be," Tim whispered back. "But you know Roger's brother? He works at the hospital and he went to the morgue and got us the real thing. I swear."

"Oh, sure," I said. But I pulled my hand away fast, accidently knocking Tim in the chin with my elbow.

"Sorry," I whispered.

I had to feel the Dead Body's eyeballs—I could tell they were peeled grapes by the smell—and walk past a ketchup-covered sheet that was supposed to be drenched in blood to get to the exit. To be honest, I was glad to be out of there!

My hands felt sticky, so I headed for the bathroom to wash them off. When I walked in, I saw a large checkered coat draped over the door of one of the stalls. I was surprised to see it there, because throwing a coat over a bathroom door is just like asking another kid to rip it off as a joke. I bent over and peeked under the door. I could see two brown loafers and the rumpled legs of a pair of yellow flannel pajamas. I stood up and looked at the coat again, considering the Great Idea that was fluttering like a bat in my belfry —the Great Idea that would make Gayle *have* to talk to me again. Slowly I tiptoed up to the stall, grabbed the coat, and whisked it off the door. I was already running out of the bathroom by the time I heard Gayle yell "Hey!"

I walked casually to the classroom, hung the coat up on a hook, and then went back to the bathroom. I began to wash my hands, humming to myself.

"Lila?" a small voice said. "It's me. Gayle."

"Oh, Gayle. Salutations."

"You have to help me," Gayle said. "Some idiot stole my coat off the door and I'm not exactly dressed underneath. Think you could try to find it for me? It's that big checkered coat of my dad's."

"I'll go *check* around," I said.

I stepped outside the bathroom for a couple of minutes, then went back in.

"No luck," I said. "Why don't you come out of there?"

"You won't believe what I have on," said Gayle grimly. The door to the bathroom stall opened slowly, revealing Gayle dressed as I knew she would be, in her faded yellow pajamas. I tried to act surprised.

Gayle slumped against the wall by the paper towel dispenser. "I didn't want to come to this stupid party tonight," she confessed. "When I got home from school, I thought I'd spend the whole evening watching this Horror Festival on TV. So I put on my pajamas and was just getting into the first movie when my mom came in and said the party was a class project and I *had* to come. She was the one who figured out this stupid costume. Finally I was so mad, I just threw it on over my pajamas and let her bring me." Gayle gave a huge sigh. "I'm really sorry I've been so horrible lately, Lila," she said. "It's just that missing trick-or-treating . . ." She shrugged her shoulders. "I look forward to it all year."

I felt like a worm! My Great Idea for the party had made my best friend totally miserable. I had to make it up to her, and I thought I knew how to do it.

"Well," I said, "unless you want to keep hiding in here, you'd better let me help you figure out another costume."

I wouldn't just go get her Sherlock coat. I'd figure out another costume for her, a better one! I stared at her and tried to think. Yellow pajamas. Fly-away yellow hair. Furry hat. What's yellow and furry? And then in a flash, I knew I could turn her into a great book character.

"I've got it," I said, as I began pulling paper towels out of the dispenser as fast as I could. "Turn your pajama top backwards and stuff these towels into the top and the pants and then tuck the top in. Wad the towels up. Like this."

Obediently Gayle headed back to the stall to make her change.

"Wait," I said. "Leave your hat with me."

While Gayle was in the bathroom, I pulled off some of the webbing that was between my ankles and knees. Then I took out my needle and thread and started sewing the yarn onto the flap of Gayle's hat. By the time Gayle came out, I was almost finished.

"Try this," I said. I put the hat on her sideways and flipped one ear flap over her forehead. The other flap went down her neck and the silvery yarn, combined with her golden hair, made a wild and woolly mane.

I yanked out some strands of webbing connecting my arms and legs and braided them together. "A tail for Gayle! Let me sew it to your rear end."

"But what about your spider costume?" asked Gayle, turning around. "What's it going to look like with half the web missing?"

Had I pulled out too much web? I looked down. Most of the yarn was still there. I'll just keep my legs together, I thought. I was sure that the originality of my costume would be obvious to the judges, even if it was a bit short on webbing.

I flipped Gayle's pajama collar up, then stood back to take a look. Stuffed with paper towels and with her blond hair billowing around her head, Gayle had *enormous* presence. I handed her three short pieces of yarn. "Tape these to your upper lip when we get to the classroom. They're your whiskers."

"Whiskers?" asked Gayle. "Okay, now tell me. What am I supposed to be?"

"Look in the mirror," I said.

Gayle went over to the big bathroom mirror. At first she just looked surprised, and then she smiled. "I look like some kind of a weird lion."

"Right!" I shouted. "From *The Wizard of Oz*! The Cowardly Lion!"

Gayle checked the mirror once more and burst out laughing. The two of us must have stood there for quite a while, laughing our heads off.

"Let's go," I said, eyeing Gayle again. It was hard to believe this lion was wearing an emergency costume. She looked perfect! "We don't want to miss the judging."

Gayle grabbed her tail and stood pigeon-toed. "I

can't go!" she wailed dramatically. "Cowards are afraid of judges!"

Then she hooked her arm through mine, and we skipped, Yellow Brick Road-style, back to the classroom. And just in the nick of time, too, because everyone was lined up for the judging. Ms. Alexander and Ms. Sherry were there, smiling and nodding, and next to them was Barney's mother, Mrs. Barker, who was one of the party chaperons.

First we all filed past the judges and then, one by one, we climbed up on a little platform to say our clue.

Michael Watson was in line in front of me. He was smeared with green makeup and had antennae shooting out from his head. He climbed onto the pedestal and raised both arms in the air. "Away, alien!" he shouted. "This planet is a peaceful place. Return to your own galaxy!"

The room was quiet. I knew no one had any idea what book character Michael was supposed to be, so I yelled out, "The Green Thing from Some Strange Planet!"

Michael turned and smiled at me. "Right. From the Planet Orkon." He stepped down.

I yanked off my glasses, pulled my ski mask from my pocket, and slid it over my head, lifting up my sweat shirt hood for an added spooky effect. Putting my spidey eyes back on, I stepped to the platform, raised my arms, and said, "Some pig!"

"Pig?" Rita Morgan wrinkled up her nose. "She looks more like some kind of disgusting insect."

"She's Charlotte!" called out Sandra. "The spider from *Charlotte's Web*!"

"You got it," I said, and struck a spidery pose. My heart was racing with excitement. I could hear the judges whispering. "Isn't that clever?" I heard Ms. Alexander say. "That one took a lot of work, too," Ms. Sherry added. Beneath my mask I smiled as I stepped off the platform. My turn for a prize was coming up.

Next Gayle stepped up. I looked over my shoulder and saw that her face was blank. And then I knew why: we hadn't figured out a line from the book for her to say!

For a split second Gayle just stood on the platform and looked uncomfortable. "Oh, gosh," she said, grabbing her tail and returning to her pigeon-toed position. "I'm afraid of judges," she said as before, batting her eyes at Ms. Alexander and Ms. Sherry, who laughed. "And little yappy dogs," Gayle went on, pretending to be crying now, and wiping her tears away with the tip of her tail. "Check these circles under my eyes," she sniveled. "I'm too scared to sleep at night. I tried counting sheep but . . . I'm terrified of sheep!"

It was a messed-up line from the movie, not the book, but nobody seemed to mind. Everyone in the room was in stitches over Gayle's performance. I was feeling happier than I had in weeks. My best friend was back.

"I know who you are!" shouted Eddie English. "The Cowardly Lion from *The Wizard of Oz!*"

Gayle looked really surprised and then she went into a shy act. "Oh, gosh," she stuttered. "I'm speechless."

Gayle stepped down, taking bows, as we all gave her a big round of applause. She had been the grand finale of the costume contest, so while the judges deliberated, we kids went to the refreshment table. There was orange juice punch, faintly orange oatmeal cake, and bright orange granola cookies dotted with black raisins. I hoped Gayle wouldn't get mad at me all over again because of having to eat health food on Halloween.

"Attention! Attention!" Mrs. Alexander called. "Gather around, boys and girls, while we announce the prizes."

I was almost shaking with excitement as we all crowded around in a big circle. Those of us with bendable costumes sat down.

"Boys and girls," Mrs. Alexander began, "we wish we could award a prize to each and every one of you. We can tell what a lot of thought and effort went into making your book character costumes. However, we have only two prizes to award."

I thought about putting my ski mask on, so I could accept my prize as a spider.

"The Best Book Character Person prize goes to Rita Morgan for her elaborate Little Bo Peep!"

Rita bounced up to Mrs. Alexander. Her costume was pretty good, with a big taffeta hoop skirt, pantaloons, and a three-foot stuffed lamb on a leash. But you would have thought that she'd won the Miss America Pageant the way she started crying and hugging Ms. Alexander. I couldn't believe it.

"Here you are, dear," said Mrs. Barker, who was handing out the prizes personally. "A movie pass for each feature film shown at the Barker Theater for one whole year."

"And now," said Ms. Alexander, "for the Best Book Character Animal."

I crossed my fingers, held my breath, and closed my eyes.

"The winner is from a classic book that most of us love to read over and over."

Come on, come on, I pleaded. *Just get to the prize.*

"And it wasn't just the costume, but the convincing acting that went with it that led us to choose . . . the Cowardly Lion. Gayle Deckert? Come up for your prize."

My eyes popped open. Wait a second, I thought. Hold it! This can't be happening! I had wanted Gayle to have a good time and get into the spirit of the party, but *I* had wanted to win.

"Here you are, dear," said Mrs. Barker, handing the prize to Gayle.

It wasn't fair! My costume was much better— much!

"We happen to be featuring *The Wizard of Oz* this

summer at the Barker Theater," Mrs. Barker went on. "I'm sure you and all your friends will want to see it."

I was a sizzling Spider of Anger! A Black Widow of poisonous thoughts! I hated this stupid Halloween party, just hated it!

Everyone gave Rita and Gayle a hand. I clapped harder than anyone, trying to hide my fury. Then we all went back to the refreshment table. A big crowd gathered around Gayle to congratulate her, which was probably a good thing, because I couldn't get close enough to her to start pouring out my angry feelings. And what good would that have done? I'd still have ended up a spider without a prize.

After we sang a few Halloween songs, the party ended. Barney Barker picked up some concrete-hard granola cookies and started throwing them like Frisbees, and just as things started to get kind of wild, Mr. Sherman announced that the party had *officially* ended.

As everyone was leaving, Gayle found me. "I'll help you with clean-up if you want," she said. "Think your mom can give me a lift home?"

I nodded, still not trusting my voice.

Cleaning up helped me forget how mad I was. Gayle held a big trash bag open while Michael and I took turns making dunk shots with the party litter. When we were finished, we went to the coat room and there, hanging innocently on a hook, was Gayle's dad's big, checkered coat.

It wasn't until we were in the backseat of my mom's car driving home that Gayle and I actually talked about what had happened.

"I think the fact that the Barker Theater is showing *The Wizard of Oz* had a lot to do with my getting a prize," said Gayle. "If they were showing *Charlotte's Web*, you'd have won."

I could tell that Gayle didn't have a clue about how much I'd wanted that prize. I half wished I could just keep it to myself, but my other half had already started talking.

"I can't believe it!" I blurted out. "Those judges— couldn't they see that this costume has everything? A spider is creepy and perfect for Halloween, *plus* Charlotte's a great book character, *plus* being a spider in the middle of a web is such an original idea! I still can't believe my costume didn't win."

"But your costume did win," said Gayle.

"What, are you nuts?" I asked.

"What won was the costume you made for me out of half of your costume."

I hadn't thought of it that way. It made me feel a little better, but not much. It was the glory of winning a prize that I'd really wanted. That and the movie pass.

Gayle and I both agreed that Eddie English should have won Rita's prize, even if Ms. Alexander had said that nursery rhymes were "cornerstones of litera-ture," and even if Eddie had gotten his character from a joke book called *I Wouldn't Send a Knight Out on a Dog Like This*.

As we approached Gayle's house, she said, "I wonder who could have taken my coat."

"Some cases are never sol—"

"Hey, Lila!" interrupted Gayle, "I just noticed something. The movie pass! Look! It says *This pass admits two patrons free*. We can both go!"

"You'll take me? Everytime you go?"

"My costume designer? But of course! Every single time," promised Gayle.

My mom pulled up in front of Gayle's house. "Thanks, Mrs. Fenwick," Gayle said. She got halfway out of the car and then turned back toward me. "Lila," she said, "you're a true friend."

A true friend, I smiled to myself, just like Charlotte.

The car door slammed, and I watched Gayle walk up the sidewalk to her front door, a lion in a checkered coat.

MY FRIEND
MICHAEL

Michael Watson's foot jiggled up and down against the metal bar under his desk, making a fidgety rattle.

"Michael!" I stage-whispered across the aisle. "Are you having a nervous breakdown or what?"

Michael peered over at me. "You're having a breakdown, Fenwick?"

"The next group may pass to the restroom," Mr. Sherman announced as three boys came back into the room. Three girls rose from their desks and walked out of the classroom door.

"Not me," I whispered back to Michael. "You! You've been jittering your stupid nerd boots on your desk all morning. Why can't you wear sneakers like a normal person?"

Michael crossed his eyes and sucked in his cheeks until he had fish lips. "I never said I was a normal person," he sputtered, sending me into a fit of giggles.

It was probably harder for Michael to wait for the last groups to come back from the bathroom than it was for any of us, because after that, we were going to line up to get on the bus that would take us on our field trip to the Museum of Natural History.

For most of us a trip to the museum meant we didn't have to sit at our desks all day, doing long division or underlining action verbs. But for Michael a trip to the Museum of Natural History was better than a trip to an ice cream factory.

Michael had been nuts about animals for as long as I could remember. And that was a long time, since his mother and my mother had become best friends when we were only a year and a half old. They met at a class for us at the Y called Tumbling Tots. I think our moms felt they had a lot in common because it was obvious from the start that Michael and I were never going to make the Toddler Olympics. Neither of us could even crawl through the Pee Wee Fun Tunnel without getting tangled up in our own legs, so our moms let us drop out of the class and we started meeting each week at the zoo. I loved seeing the animals, but Michael not only loved them, he became an expert on them right away. No kidding. He could tell you the difference between a jaguar and a leopard before he was out of diapers.

"While we're waiting for the next group to return

from the restroom, let's review what we know about food chains," said Mr. Sherman. "Who can name a grass-eating animal?"

"Rabbit," Michael called out.

"And who can name a predator, or an animal that preys on rabbits for food?"

"Hawk," said Michael.

"Okay, grass, rabbit, hawk: three links of a food chain," said Mr. Sherman. "Now, can anyone *besides* Michael tell me what might happen in a very dry year, when the grass doesn't grow well?"

"My dad would make me get up early to set the sprinklers," said Barney Barker, trying to look innocent.

"What might happen to our *food chain* in a dry year?" Mr. Sherman looked as if he'd had a long day already.

"The rabbits wouldn't have enough to eat," said Michael, "and many of them would die, which would make less food for hawks."

Lynn Williamson, Sandra Guth, and Kelly MacConnell walked in from the girl's room and the last group of boys, Tim Petefish, Roger Rupp, and Barney Barker, got up from their desks and headed for the door. Barney walked with his legs squeezed together, as if he might not make it to the bathroom in time.

"So why don't hawks die out, too, in a drought year?" asked Mr. Sherman, continuing his line of questioning.

"Some do," Michael answered. "But hawks also eat animals that don't depend on grass for food, such as snakes and frogs and even insects. Hawks can adapt to a dry year by seeking other kinds of food— or even new kinds."

"They'd *adapt*," repeated Mr. Sherman. "Does everyone understand how important it is that animals have the ability to *adapt* or adjust to changes in their environment?"

We all nodded, hoping that none of us would be called on to explain just how important it was.

"This is how they survive!" Mr. Sherman stood up to make his point just as the last three boys came back from the john.

"Before you line up to get on the bus, there's something I want to give each of you." Mr. Sherman loved to be mysterious. In his hands he held a pack of post cards, and he walked around the room, holding the cards fanned out, blank side up, asking us all to pick one but to leave it facedown on our desks until everyone in the class had a card.

"Now, turn the cards up," said Mr. Sherman.

I flipped my card and found myself looking into the face of a great horned owl. Not a bad pick, I thought. A wise old owl was just the animal to inspire me with a Great Idea for my report.

I looked around to see what other kids had gotten. Michael had a long, thin weasely animal on his card. In front of me Sandra Guth was holding a card with some sort of squirrel on it. I felt bad for her, getting stuck with an animal you could see in the schoolyard any old day. But at least she didn't have what Rita Morgan was staring at on her card—a brown rat!

"Each of you now has your assignment, which will complete our study of animal food chains," explained Mr. Sherman. "Think of yourselves as specializing in the animal on your card. When we get to the museum, you are to find the exhibit on your animal and get as much information as you can on what it eats and what, if anything, eats it. Find out about at least one food chain your animal fits into. When we return to school, some of you may want to gather more facts from libary research, but those of you who use your time at the museum well may have your reports complete as you get back on the bus. Any questions?"

Barney Barker raised his hand. Mr. Sherman looked pleased that Barney was interested enough in food chains to ask a question.

"Are we going to the gift shop?" Barney asked, pulling a five dollar bill from between the pages of his math book and waving it in the air.

"The gift shop," Mr. Sherman said, sighing, "will be our last stop at the museum. Those of you who would like to do so can purchase a souvenir at that time. Any questions pertaining to your animals?"

"Can we trade our animal cards if we want to?" asked Rita Morgan. I wondered who she thought would trade her for the brown rat.

"No," said Mr. Sherman. "It's the luck of the draw today. If there are no more questions, you may get your coats and quietly line up at the door with a partner."

Gayle was absent today, so I was without my usual partner. "Michael!" I called on the way to the coatroom. "Let's be partners!" Michael usually got stuck being partners with Jason Johnson, known in our class for having killer halitosis. I figured I'd be a welcome relief.

"I've already got one, Fenwick," Michael said, brushing past me to get in line. "Better luck next time."

"Better luck yourself." It was hard to believe Michael would actually choose to sit next to Jason on a bus with closed windows. I scanned the coatroom for a partner and there, to my surprise, was Jason, obviously looking around for a partner, too. So who could Michael's partner be, I wondered? Desperately I searched the coatroom for someone else without a partner and spotted Rita standing next to Roger's mother, the trip chaperone. Even Miss Perfect would make a better partner than Reptile Breath.

Without wasting another second I walked up to Rita. "I haven't got a partner," I said. "Have you?"

"I thought I'd sit next to Mrs. Rupp," explained Rita, winking up at Roger's mom.

"Oh, I didn't realize there were other children who hadn't been paired up, Rita. You two go ahead and be partners," said Roger's mother, backing away from Rita rather eagerly, I thought. "I'll sit with Mr. Sherman."

"This field trip," muttered Rita, more to herself than to her new partner, "is really the pits."

Near the end of the line I saw Michael and Eddie English standing together. So that was his partner! Eddie English! How odd. Michael and Eddie had been in the same class since kindergarten, but this was the first time I'd ever seen them talking to each other. Now good old Michael was jabbering away as if nothing were unusual. He never seemed to notice Jason Johnson's bad breath, and now he didn't seem to notice that he was partners with the most popular boy in the class. Nothing seemed to matter to Michael when there were animals to discuss. Roger Rupp and Tim Petefish were behind Michael and Eddie in line. The four of them were talking and laughing like crazy.

Two by two we filed out the classroom door into the bitterly cold January air, and onto the big yellow bus. Inside it smelled of ripe bananas and old bologna sandwiches.

"Take the seat farthest back to make room for others," said Mr. Sherman, waving his arm in that direction.

"There's no way I can sit in the back of this bus," Rita announced as she climbed up the steps.

"No exceptions," said Mr. Sherman. He kept waving. "Each of you is to take the seat closest to the back when you get on."

"I have this incredibly delicate stomach, Mr. Sherman," Rita went on. "If I have to sit anywhere *near* the back of a bus and get, you know, bounced around? I could get, like, cosmically ill. Really."

"Take the front seat, Rita." Mr. Sherman knew when he was beaten. "And remember to open the window and get some fresh air if you feel like you're going to vomit."

Everyone started giggling and making gagging signs, but Rita just ignored them as she sat down in the best seat on the bus. As the bus pulled out of the parking lot, Rita pulled an emery board out of her purse and began filing her nails.

Directly behind me I heard Michael and Eddie talking. I turned around. "What animal have you got, Michael?"

But Michael didn't seem to hear me. "Your lynx," he was telling Eddie, "is an incredible hunter. In the winter most other big cats sink in the deep snow, but the lynx can walk right on top of it because it has these huge feet that act like snowshoes."

"It's Big Foot of the Forest!" shouted Roger from the seat across from Eddie and Michael.

"Yeah," chimed in Tim. "The Abominable Snow Lynx!"

"Hey, Michael!" I tried again.

But both Michael and Eddie were laughing so hard they must have been drowning out any other sounds.

"And it doesn't hunt by chasing its prey," Michael went on in a minute. "What it likes to do is lie on a tree branch, totally still, and wait for an unsuspecting animal to walk right under it and POW! The lynx pounces on it, and before the animal even knows what hit it, the lynx breaks its neck."

"Talk about fast food," said Roger.

"Well," said Michael, "if the animal had been faster, it wouldn't have ended up as food!"

There was another round of laughs. Those guys sounded to me like a bunch of second graders. Then Eddie asked, "About how big is a full-grown lynx?"

"It's ninety to one hundred pounds in this country and bigger in Canada, where the lynx actually hunts reindeer."

I turned toward Rita. Her nails were evidently finished, for she was now gazing out the window of the bus. She nodded her head at a shopping mall we were passing. "I wish we could stop off here," she told me. "They've got these really outrageous sweaters at The Fashion Bee right now."

"Un-*bee*-lievable," I answered.

"Really," Rita replied.

That was about all Rita and I had to say to each other, so I just leaned back in my seat and listened to Michael telling Eddie everything he'd ever need to know about his lynx. "The biggest predator of the lynx is man," he was saying. "A lynx has very sensitive hearing and can protect itself against enemies that move through the brush, but it can't protect itself against a silent trap."

The way Michael talked about that lynx made *me* want to know all about it, even if it wasn't the animal on my card. I remembered once, when we were in first grade, Michael had become fascinated by Huggins, this huge boa constrictor in the zoo's Reptile House. I thought snakes were creepy, but Michael kept telling me about Huggins. He made me see how quiet and calm the boa was, how funny it looked taking a nap with its eyes open, how it liked to be held and would wind slowly around its zookeeper's arm up to his shoulder, sniffing with its narrow, Y-shaped tongue. It wasn't long before I was as excited as Michael about our weekly visits to see that snake.

Michael loved animals so much that, when he started talking about them, he made you love them, too. He sure was making Eddie curious about his lynx. Eddie was learning more about his animal on the bus than he would in the museum!

Suddenly a terrible thought came to me. What if Eddie was just using Michael to help him with his report? What if that was why he picked him for a partner?

I tuned in on the conversation behind me once more.

"Does the lynx eat the same things in the summer as he does in the winter?" Eddie asked.

I could see it now—Eddie English getting extra credit for reporting on both the lynx's summer food chain and its winter one. This was too much! My friend Michael was being used for his smarts by Eddie English—and he didn't even have the brains to figure out what was going on.

I folded my arms across my chest and sat in my bus

seat fuming. Eddie English, Chocolate Eyes! Eddie English, T.K.O.! The truth was, Eddie English was nothing but a creep.

Just then the bus bumped over a few bad spots in the road. Rita leaped up, half out of her seat, and struggled to open the window.

Oh, no, I thought. A couple of potholes and the Delicate Stomach is about to blow breakfast on the bus. I jumped up to help Rita open the window, but as I did, the bus came to a sudden stop and I bashed my forehead on the silvery post in front of me. Grabbing the post to keep my balance, I swung all the way out of my seat into the aisle. I looked up and found myself facing my whole class, everyone staring at me. I did the only thing I could think of: I took a bow.

The bus had arrived in the museum parking lot.

"Boys and girls," announced Mr. Sherman, "you will file quietly out the door and wait in line beside the bus until everyone is ready to go inside."

And so we piled out of the bus. Eddie and Michael were right behind Rita and me, still talking a mile a minute about Eddie's lynx.

I tried not to do it, I really tried, but I couldn't help myself. I turned around to Eddie.

"Why bother to go into the museum at all, Eddie?" I asked, in a voice as phony-sweet as I could make it. "Sounds to me like you've got enough material for your report already. *More* than enough."

Eddie looked surprised and a little confused. He

shrugged his shoulders at Michael. Michael just smiled his out-of-it smile at both of us.

"What animal have you got, Fenwick?" Michael asked.

I flashed my card at him. "Great horned owl."

Barney Barker snuck up behind me. "Hoot! Hoot!" he shouted in my ear. "Lila's got horns! Lila's got horns!" Everyone around me laughed.

Rita had been right about one thing: this field trip was really the pits. I was freezing and my nose was starting to drip. A lump of gray snow had dropped into my sneaker as I stepped off the bus, soaking my sock. Beneath my bangs my forehead was throbbing where I had hit it on the pole. I would have to put up with Miss Perfect for at least three more hours. And what if the Delicate Stomach threw up on me on the bus ride home.

At last Mr. Sherman led us across the slushy parking lot and into the door of the museum. We hung up our jackets and waited in the high-ceilinged lobby as Mr. Sherman and Mrs. Rupp shook hands with a pale, slender woman in a red Museum Guide smock.

"This is Ms. Fox," announced Mr. Sherman. "She will lead our tour today."

I wondered if all the museum guides had names like hers. If we came again, would our tour be led by Mr. Baboon? Or Ms. Wombat?

"Welcome, everyone, to the Museum of Natural History," said Ms. Fox, looking, with her strawberry-blond hair and small, pointed face, very much like her name. "I understand that your teacher has arranged a Food Chain Hunt for you today. I'll just give you a quick tour of the museum so that you can find your way around. Let's get started."

Our guide led us briskly through a wide doorway. I noticed that if I squinted through my bangs at Ms. Fox, some of her human features blurred and she looked even foxier.

"This exhibit shows animals of the order Carnivora," explained Ms. Fox. "Do any of you know what carnivores are?"

"Meat eaters," volunteered Michael.

We stopped beside a glass case holding a weasel. Its mouth was open in a snarl, showing its large, canine teeth.

"Check those fangs," Roger whispered to Tim. "Looks like a vampire weasel!"

Ms. Fox evidently had good ears, for she said, "Those teeth do look lethal, don't they? Weasels kill small animals by biting them in the neck, but they don't suck their blood."

"This animal is totally ugly," said Rita with a show-off shudder. "Beyond skinny."

I squinched my eyes almost closed and tried to see Rita as a snarling weasel. It wasn't all that hard.

"Well," said Ms. Fox, "a weasel's body needs to be slender so that it can fit down mouse and mole holes to find its prey. A pleasingly plump weasel wouldn't live very long, I'm afraid. Every animal must adapt itself to live and eat the best it can in its particular home. You may not think a weasel's pretty, but it has a very functional look for the job it has to do."

Eyes still squinted, I checked out Eddie. I tried to see him as the skunk he was, but his oversized brown eyes kept making me see him as a deer.

Michael raised his hand. Ms. Fox nodded at him. "I read once about a type of goat that lived on a special kind of grass."

Michael was easy to squint into an animal, but not one that would be on display at the museum: a stray cat—skinny, alert, and uncombed.

"But people moved into the goats' territory," Michael was saying, "and farms began taking up the goats' pasture land, so the goats had to move higher and higher up a mountain in order to find their grass. Up in the high altitudes the air was very thin, so this kind of goat developed extra-big lungs that could breathe easily there."

"That's an excellent example of animals adapting," said Ms. Fox. "All animals have this power to adjust to changes in their living conditions. Animals that can adapt the best will thrive in new situations, but animals that can't adapt will die out sooner or later."

Eyes narrowed, I watched a hefty brown bear come toward me.

"Lila, is the low lighting bothering your eyes?" Mr. Sherman's whisper seemed a low growl. "You've been squinting terribly ever since we got here."

"My eyes?" I opened them wide. "No, they're okay." But on this rotten day I felt I could use a little sympathy, so I added, "My dad has really bad eyes. I guess I've inherited them." I squinted up at him, adding, "Maybe it's the beginning of pink eye or a sty or . . ."

Instead of looking sympathetic, Mr. Sherman looked amused. "Shall I take you to the first aid station here, or are you starting to feel better now?" He certainly had a way of putting things clearly.

"Much better," I said, springing my eyes wide open and running to catch up with the rest of the class.

We were led on, then, past the weasel, past a red fox, a coyote, and a crouching lynx, which made me feel mad at Eddie all over again. In a minute we left the mammals and went through the Hall of Birds, where I caught just a glimpse of my owl.

Sly Ms. Fox took us quickly through the whole museum, and finally back to the lobby where we began.

Brown Bear Sherman called us to attention.

"Now you know the lay of the land," he began. "Stay with your partner and take turns gathering information on where your animal fits into a food chain. Any questions?" Everybody was itching to go their separate ways, so no one had any questions.

"Shall we go dig up some info on your beast first?" I asked Rita.

She nodded. "Let's get this over with."

We went past the carnivores to the exhibit on small mammals and found her brown rat.

"Why don't I read you the information from the poster and you can take notes?" I suggested.

"Excellent." Rita opened her notebook and pulled out her pink unicorn pen with the strawberry-scented ink.

"Rita, don't you have anything else to write with? A plain old Bic maybe? That chemical strawberry smell is gross."

Rita looked surprised that anyone could find her smelly pen offensive. She checked her pencil case and held up a fat purple pen. "You like grape better?"

"Doesn't matter," I said, wondering if I could hold my breath and read at the same time. "Here goes. 'No animal is more adaptable than the Brown Rat. It can be found from beach areas to mountain peaks, from farms to factories.' "

"Slow down," commanded Rita. "I'm not a computer."

"You could write faster if you don't dot your *i*'s with little circles," I informed her.

Somehow we made it through the information chart. Rita had to write down a long list of animals who lived on brown rats, but luckily none of the predators had any *i*'s in their names: dogs, cats, weasels, martens, foxes, otters, eagles, buzzards, herons, and, I was pleased to find, owls.

When we finished, Rita pulled a Lo-cal Banana Bar out of her purse. "I'm starving," she said. "Want some?"

"Not right now," I said. The combined smells of artificial banana flavor and strawberry ink made me feel like I might develop a Delicate Stomach. I guess Rita saw the look on my face.

"This is the only thing my mom lets me snack on," she told me. "We're all on this high energy fruit diet right now, and this Banana Bar counts as one fruit."

At that moment I actually felt sorry for Rita. Her mother had her whole family on one disgusting diet after another. But still it made me nervous, Rita eating. Even a fruit bar. Would it stay down on the bus ride home? Maybe I could arrange things so that Rita sat directly behind Eddie English. It made me feel better just to picture him with a half-digested banana bar splatting onto the back of his neck.

Rita read over her notes as she chewed. "That poster listed all the animals that, you know, eat this disgusting rat. But it didn't really tell what the disgusting rat eats."

I skimmed the information again. "You're right."

"Michael probably knows. We could ask him," said Rita, popping the last of the banana bar into her mouth. "He is so in touch when it comes to animals."

"Forget Michael," I said. "He's so busy being Eddie's new best friend he probably wouldn't have time to tell you."

"Really." Rita gave me a weird look. "Well, let's go find your owl. Maybe we'll, like, run into Ms. Fox on the way, and I can ask her about it."

We entered the Hall of Birds and went right to my huge owl, with his great, moon-shaped face and wicked hooked claws. His horns looked like feathered ears on top of his head.

"My turn to read," said Rita.

I got out my notebook and said, "Sh-HOOT."

" 'The Great Horned Owl lives alone and hunts for food at night. Its powerful wings allow it to fly almost silently through the night, swooping down on its prey. Among its favorite prey is the pine marten.' "

It was almost shocking to hear Rita's voice producing regular English sentences as she read all about my owl. Its great big eyes let it see in the dark about a hundred times better than humans. But it was disappointing to find out that owls aren't really wise at all. It's just their big eyes that make them look that way. In fact, an owl's eyes weigh more than its brain!

When Rita finished reading, we decided to go check out the pine marten to complete my information on the owl's food chain, so we headed back to the Carnivora Room. There we found the pine marten. We also found Michael and Eddie sprawled out around the pine marten case. Michael was writing furiously in his notebook.

"Hi, Eddie," Rita crooned. "Hi, Michael."

"Hi, Michael," I said, ignoring Eddie. And then

suddenly I realized what Michael was doing. "Is this your animal? The pine marten?"

Michael nodded, still writing.

"Guess what?" I said. "Your animal is my animal's favorite food!"

Michael looked up at me. "You have the great horned owl?"

"Right."

"That's funny," said Eddie. "My animal—"

"I don't think there's anything so funny about it," I snapped.

"I wasn't finished," said Eddie flatly. Then he looked at me, stared at me with those deer eyes. Cow eyes, I told myself. Water buffalo eyes.

"Could I talk to you a minute, Lila?" Eddie said. "Over here." He was walking toward the side of the exhibit room, near a drinking fountain.

Before I could think how to say no, I was walking over to the drinking fountain, too. If this had happened yesterday, I would have been thrilled that Eddie wanted to talk to me. But now I was only mad, mad, MAD!

Eddie turned to face me. "Look, Lila," he said, "I figured out what you meant. What you said outside. You think I'm using Michael to do my report for me."

"That's right," I told him. "I do."

"Well I'm not," said Eddie.

"Oh, I suppose it's just a coincidence that you picked him for your partner for the Museum of

Natural History trip? Would you have picked him for the field trip to the art museum?"

Eddie's eyes opened even wider than usual. "Lila, maybe you should get the facts straight before you go around accusing people of things. I didn't pick Michael for a partner—he picked me."

Now it was my turn to open my eyes wide. "Michael asked you to be his partner?"

"That's right," said Eddie.

"When?"

"This morning. Before school. We were talking about the trip out by the crosswalk." Eddie gave me a funny little smile. "Maybe the real reason you're so mad is that you just can't stand the thought that Michael might have other friends besides you."

"What?" I couldn't believe what I was hearing.

"Yeah, Lila," Eddie went on. "Were you ever mad when Michael got stuck with Jason Johnson as a partner? If you're such a good friend of Michael's, how come *you* never pick him as a partner?"

"I asked him to be my partner," I said smugly. "Today."

"Right," said Eddie. "But only because Gayle was absent."

I felt my anger turning to confusion. I just stood there by the drinking fountain, letting Eddie's words fall into place. Was it true, I wondered? Was I angry because I'd felt left out on the bus? Because I was stuck with the humorless Rita while Michael and his friends were having so much fun together? Did I want things to stay just the way they'd always been? Michael with his nose in his sci-fi and animal books, totally out of it and yet always there, always available to be my friend when I needed him? Maybe. Maybe I did.

I looked over at Michael. He was squatting on the floor, writing in his notebook. Just then he finished and looked over at us.

"The two deadly predators in conference," he called. "It's curtains for the pine marten." He pretended to choke himself with both hands.

"Two predators?" I was puzzled.

"That's what I was about to tell you before," said Eddie as we started walking back over to the display case. "The pine marten is also the favorite food of the lynx—my animal."

"Oh." I couldn't say anything else. I was thinking. If an animal's environment changed, it adapted. Either that, or it died out. Well, things around here were changing. Michael was making friends with Eddie and Roger and Tim. It was easy to see that they really liked him, and why shouldn't they? Michael was smart and funny and interesting. But I liked him a lot, too! Why hadn't I showed it more? I didn't want my friendship with him to die out just because he had made some new friends. If weasels and mice and owls and goats could adjust to changes in the balance of things, well, I guessed I could, too.

I walked over to Michael beside the pine marten case and gave him a little pinch on his scrawny cheek.

"This pine marten looks particularly delicious," I said to Eddie. "Maybe the owl and the lynx should agree to split him."

"It's a deal," said Eddie, and he reached out to shake my hand. It might have been my imagination, but it seemed like Eddie shook my hand a little longer than necessary to seal the deal.

Rita had been standing beside Michael, telling him what cosmic notes he was taking, while she kept her eyes glued to Eddie.

"I don't feel quite so bad anymore," Michael told us, smiling at Rita. "Guess who's at the bottom of this food chain? The brown rat!"

"Can you believe it, Eddie?" Rita said brightly. "Our animals are in the same food chain!"

Maybe it was Rita's superb acting ability that was responsible for the Great Idea that hit me then and there with the force of a great horned owl swooping down on its prey.

"I've got a Great Idea," I said.

"Oh, no!" wailed Michael, Eddie, and Rita all together. But secretly they wanted to know what it was. I made them drag it out of me.

"It's our reports," I said finally. "We could do them together, as a play."

"Food Chain Theater presents . . . 'You Are What You Eat,'" goofed Michael. "Brought to you by the Predator Insurance Group." He bent his fingers into menacing claws. "The kind of protection only a predator can guarantee."

"And now our program," said Eddie, imitating a radio announcer's voice.

I loved it!

"You'd start it off, Rita," I directed, "as the brown rat. You want to do it with us? As a play?"

Poor Rita! She looked as if the Delicate Stomach might act up any second. Here was her chance to work on a project with Eddie English, T.K.O., but to do it, she'd have to play a rat!

"Well," I went on, "if you want to, you'd tell all about yourself and what you eat, and what you're scared might eat you, and then, just as you're finishing, Michael, the pine marten, pounces in, knocks you offstage, and begins his report."

"Maybe you can borrow my mom's old fur coat for the part, Rita," offered Eddie.

"Fur coat!" exclaimed Rita. "You mean, real fur? For real?"

"Well, it is pretty ratty," said Eddie. "That's why I suggested it for your part."

"Fur coats," muttered Michael, frowning. "Last week I saw someone wearing a leopard coat. It's just hard to imagine such total insensitivity to the environment and to the possible extinction of literally hundreds of endangered species."

"For sure," chimed in the adaptable Rita.

The four of us sat there plotting and planning our play until Mr. Sherman came by, announcing that it was time to gather in the museum cafeteria for lunch.

The rest of our field trip seemed to zoom by. In the

cafeteria we had boxed lunches of bologna and cheese sandwiches with cartons of room-temperature milk. After that we trooped up to the gift shop. Barney Barker bought a two-foot model of a stegosaurus for $4.98, and then broke it when he sat on it on the bus ride home. Michael, Eddie, Rita, and I were still brainstorming our report as we climbed back on to the bus. and Rita forgot to demand the front seat. Yet somehow, even though the bus jolted, jittered, and jounced us, the Delicate Stomach did not complain. Not so much as a growl. You might even say it adapted.

THE BET

"Watch," said Sandra Guth as she held the flat stone between her thumb and first finger. She swung her arm back and then whipped it forward, with just a flick of the wrist as she let the stone go, and it skipped once, twice, three times—four, five times!—over the surface of Weekeegan Pond.

I had to admit it was impressive.

"Look for stones that are nice and flat," she said to the rest of us. "They're the easiest to skip."

We all searched the bank of the pond for flat stones while we waited for Sandra's mother and Lynn's mother, our camp leaders. They were checking in with the director of Camp Weekeegan, where we had just arrived for a Fifth Grade Girls' Spring Weekend.

All the fifth graders in our city took turns coming to Weekeegan. It was Saturday morning and we were going to stay until Sunday night doing what my father called "roughing it."

"How's this one?" asked Rita, holding up a teensy white rock.

"A bit on the small side," said Sandra. "But try it."

Rita closed one eye, squinched up her face, and threw the stone, which landed in the pond with a single soft plop.

"Wow!" I shouted, bobbing my head up and down, pretending to watch the stone skip a dozen times over the water. "It's a new world's record!"

Rita whirled around. "Very funny, Lila. Why don't you try it, you know? I bet you can't do any better."

"Just joking, Rita," I said. "Don't take it so hard."

But Rita inched up closer to me. Those big blue eyes that she usually held so wide open were now angry little slits.

"You try it, Lila," she repeated. "I bet you can't do it either. I bet you a dollar."

Rita knew I had a dollar because our parents had all agreed that we could each spend one dollar, no more, on candy at the Camp Weekeegan Canteen.

"Take the bet," said Sandra. "It's easy."

Easy for you, I thought. I'd never skipped a stone in my life. But the pressure was on.

"Okay, Rita," I said. "It's a bet."

I looked around for the best rock I could find and

came up with one that was flat as a pancake, even if it was pretty good-sized.

"Hold your arm out, almost straight," said Sandra, "and then wham it forward."

"No coaching!" shouted Rita.

It was very quiet. I stood there for a moment, feeling the weight of the rock in my hand and the eyes of each girl watching me. "I am *not* a klutz. I am *not* a klutz," I silently chanted. Then I brought my arm back and flung it out hard—too hard! My body began spinning around and I let go of the rock —too late. Instead of hearing my stone skipping over the top of the pond, instead of hearing a loud plink as my stone sank into the water, we heard a musical tinkling sound.

"Uh-oh," said Gayle. "Look."

She pointed to a small basement window in the Weekeegan dining lodge, just behind the pond. The glass had been shattered and what was left of the window was hanging in jagged pieces.

"Serves you right, Lila." Rita was smiling now. "You still owe me a dollar."

That was the least of my worries, because just then I saw Mrs. Guth and Mrs. Williamson coming out of the lodge. From the look on Mrs. Williamson's face, I guessed that she had heard the glass break.

"What's going on here, girls?" Mrs. Williamson towered over us. "Can't we trust you to behave yourselves for five minutes?" Quickly she looked along the wall of the lodge and found the splintered window. "Who is responsible for this?"

I took a deep breath and raised my hand.

"Lila Fenwick, how did you break the window?" Mrs. Williamson demanded.

"A rock," I said. "By accident."

Mrs. Williamson pointed a long finger at the broken window. "Accidents like this don't just happen. You girls wait here. Thelma," she said to Mrs. Guth, "you'd better wait with them to see that there are no more accidents. I'll go back to the lodge and see what Ms. Gupton wants to do about this."

As Mrs. Williamson headed back to the lodge, Mrs. Guth came up beside me and put her arm around my shoulder. "Don't worry," she said.

"What if they ask us to leave camp?" Rita asked, not looking entirely upset by the idea.

"No one's going to ask us to leave, Rita," said Mrs. Guth. "It's only a little window."

I sat down on a large rock to wait and see what would happen next. To my surprise Lynn Williamson sat down next to me. I'd been in school with her since we were five years old, and I'd hardly ever heard her say a word. Now that I'd met her mother, I began to understand why.

"I'm sorry my mom got so mad," said Lynn.

"Yeah." I shrugged. "It's not your fault."

Together we watched as the door of the lodge opened once again. Mrs. Williamson charged out.

"Lila!" she called. "The camp director would like

to speak with you. Her office is at the far end of the lodge."

Gayle nudged me. "I'll come with you, if you want."

"Thanks," I whispered.

The two of us started up the lodge path.

"Gayle!" Mrs. Williamson called. "Ms. Gupton wants to see Lila. Alone."

"Oh, Victoria," said Mrs. Guth to Mrs. Williamson. "What harm is there in them going together?" And then she called to us, "Hurry, girls. Let's get this over with."

Gayle and I ran up the path before Mrs. Williamson could say anything to stop us.

I pulled open the wide wooden door of the lodge and we stepped inside. The high windows let very little light into this enormous cave of a room. Chairs and benches stacked high on tables looked like unsteady stalactites. "What do you think the camp director will say?" I asked.

Gayle rubbed her hands together in ghoulish delight. "Well, dearie," she began, her camp director voice sounding exactly like the Wicked Witch of the West, "we have a special cabin for bad campers like you, who destroy our property. You don't mind spending the night with a few toads and snakes and bats, do you, my pretty?"

Grimly I faced a door with an ancient, woodburned sign saying CAMP DIRECTOR. I swallowed hard and knocked.

"Come in!" boomed a hearty voice.

Slowly I pushed open the door and saw a cluttered desk with a big woman sitting behind it. She had short hair, big dark eyes, and around her neck on a braided blue and yellow lanyard hung a worn silver whistle.

"Don't just stand there, come on in!" With a friendly wave she motioned us into her disorderly office. "I'm Ms. Gupton, better known around here as Guppy." She stood and reached her big hand out over her desk to shake our hands.

I felt the little knot that had been tying itself in my stomach begin to loosen.

"I'm Lila Fenwick," I spoke up. "This is my friend Gayle Deckert. I'm the one who broke the window. By accident."

"So you broke the window," said Guppy. She sat down and leaned back in her chair. "Let me ask you something, campers. Do you think this is the first time something like this has ever happened at Camp Weekeegan?"

"I—I guess so," I said. "I'm very sorry about it."

"Well," said Guppy, "let me assure you that this is not the first time, nor will it be the last, that one of those little windows has been broken. In fact," she went on, "they get broken—by accident—so regularly that I happen to know a new pane costs exactly ten dollars."

It took me a second to realize what she was getting at.

"I'll pay for the new glass," I said.

"That would be fine. Good enough." Guppy leaned forward in her chair again. She seemed as relieved as I was that this discussion was about to end. "When you get home, just have your parents send me a check for ten dollars, and don't give this incident another thought. You're here to have a good time!"

"Thank you, Guppy," I said.

"If you need anything, campers, just ask. You know where to find me." Guppy stood up behind her desk. She put out her hand and we shook it again.

"That wasn't so bad," said Gayle as we headed back outside.

"Not as bad as it could have been," I admitted. "But I'll have to pay my parents back for the window."

"How many weeks allowance will it take you?"

"Well, I get two-fifty a week," I said, "so it would take a month."

"*Would*?" asked Gayle.

"It would," I said, "if I hadn't just arranged to borrow five months of my allowance in advance to make up the difference in price for the bike my parents were willing to buy me and the bike I wanted. This would make me six months in debt to my mom and dad. They'll never go for it. I'm sure they'll say the bike deal is off. Unless . . ."

"Unless what?"

"Unless I can figure out some other way to get the money."

Ten dollars. That number kept knocking around in my head as we picked up our sleeping bags and knapsacks and hiked to Bat Bungalow, the cabin between Chipmunk Cottage and Robins' Roost, that we were to have for the weekend. Bat Bungalow was a plain, high-ceilinged wooden building holding a dozen bunk beds with thin blue- and white-striped mattresses. There was no electricity, so after dark we'd have to use our flashlights to get around. I was happy to find out that the cabin had an indooor bathroom, even though Rita claimed to have seen a spider the size of a kitten on the toilet seat.

Mrs. Williamson and Mrs. Guth had a separate room, which was really only semi-private because its partitions stopped about six inches from the floor and didn't go up anywhere near the ceiling. I guessed that it gave grown-ups who chaperoned camping trips just a little bit of kid-free space.

Gayle and I flipped a coin to see who would get top bunk. As usual, Gayle won, so I unrolled my sleeping bag on the bottom. On our bedside stand Gayle and I set out our flashlights, toothbrushes, toothpaste, plastic cups, hairbrushes, combs, and Gayle's retainer case, while on the stand next to ours, Rita unpacked her giant-sized can of insect repellant, Powder Pink nail polish, polish remover, cotton balls, skin moisturizer, and paper toilet seat covers.

When we were finished settling in, Mrs. Williamson called us together for a little meeting to go over camp rules and regulations. She concluded by saying, "And, while we're here at camp, we're going to let you girls call us by our nicknames."

"When I was young," said Mrs. Guth, "I used to be called Shorty. I have no idea why."

Everyone laughed. Mrs. Guth wasn't much taller than your average fifth grader.

"And I was called Cricket," announced Mrs. Williamson. "Probably because I had a cheerful voice."

No one laughed this time. Mrs. Williamson— *Cricket*? I had a funny feeling that no one had ever called her by a nickname in her life; that she was making up this nickname for herself. But why? I wondered. So that we'd like her more? I looked across the circle at Lynn. She was staring at her hands in her lap.

After the meeting we went on a nature hike. Mrs. Williamson looked like she'd stepped right out of a page of the L.L.Bean Outdoors Catalog, with binoculars around her neck, a jackknife dangling from a belt loop of her khaki shorts, and heavy, cleated hiking boots. My class identified five kinds of birds and twenty-three different kinds of trees, while I tried, without any luck, to identify just one Great Idea for making ten dollars.

On the way back to Bat Bungalow a tree branch tripped me and I found myself sprawled belly down on the trail. Lying there, so close to nature, I noticed that a rock about an inch from my nose had a leaf marking on it. As I picked myself up, I picked it up, too, and showed it to Mrs. Williamson.

"It's a fossil," Mrs. Williamson exclaimed.

Suddenly Rita began pointing at the rock, jumping up and down. "Oh! Shorty! Mrs. Williamson! Look at the bottom of that rock! There's some kind of slimy creature!"

Shorty peered at the rock. "Well, Rita, you've just identified our first leach."

"Yuk!" said Mrs. Williamson. Holding the rock with her fingertips, she scraped it against a tree and squished the leach all over the bark.

"Dis-gusting!" said Gayle.

"Some nature lover," I added.

When the hike was over, we went back to our cabin to wash up, and then to the lodge for dinner. Our class sat together at one long table. Mrs. Williamson told us to use our best Price School table manners to set an example for the campers from other schools.

"May I please have the salt, Mrs. Williamson?" asked Kelly MacConnell politely.

"Cricket," Mrs. Williamson reminded her, passing the shaker.

"Blech!" Gayle made a face as she tasted the meat loaf. "This is horrible. And sliced beets! I hope the dessert's better."

"I bet you do," said Rita from across the table,

puffing out her cheeks in imitation of Gayle's round face. Rita was daintily nibbling away at the grapefruit, Baco-Bits, and spinach salad that her mother had packed for her to bring to camp in a baggie.

Gayle glowered at Rita.

"Never mind," I whispered to my friend. "Rita wouldn't know good food if it hit her in the face."

I looked down at the sliver of beet in my spoon and then over at Rita.

Gayle watched me, wide-eyed. "You wouldn't dare."

"Wanna bet?" I asked, forgetting for the moment that I was already in enough trouble to last me the rest of the camping trip. I waited until no one was looking, then flipped the beet across the table. It landed with a satisfying smack on Rita's neck. "Flying leaches!" Gayle cried out, which is probably why Rita began screaming at the top of her lungs. If she hadn't screamed, Kelly MacConnell probably wouldn't have jumped to her feet so suddenly and knocked the pitcher of milk all over the table.

I think we all expected Mrs. Williamson to get angry and yell, but she didn't. She just sat there, looking at us as though she couldn't believe her eyes, while a puddle of milk near her elbow dripped steadily onto her hiking shorts.

We Price School girls had certainly set an interesting example of table manners for the campers from other schools.

After dinner we had free time until campfire at 7:00. Gayle and I walked back to a clearing on the nature trail and sat on a couple of smooth brown rocks still warm from the sun.

"You're awfully quiet," Gayle said.

"I'm thinking," I told her. "I've got a Great Idea skipping around in my head. I can feel it. I'm just about to think of a way to make ten bucks."

We sat there together on our rocks, thinking. Then Gayle started to giggle.

"It was so great at dinner! I can still see that beet, thwack, right on the old Adam's apple!" Gayle's laugh was so contagious, I started laughing, too. "You may not be able to skip a rock, Fenwick, but you sure can flip a vegetable!" The giggles overcame Gayle again. "I would gladly have paid you a dollar for that beet shot. You should have made it a real bet."

"A real bet," I repeated. The Great Idea was skimming the surface of my brain more slowly now.

"You know," said Gayle. "You said, 'Wanna bet?' and then you bonged the beet and then—"

"A real bet," I interrupted. The Great Idea stopped skipping and began to sink in.

Gayle looked at me closely. "You okay, Lila?"

I jumped off my rock. "How many of us are on this campout?"

"Every girl in our class is here," said Gayle, "except Barbara, so that makes fourteen."

"That's thirteen, not counting me," I said. "What if . . . what if . . ." And I explained to Gayle my stunning Great Idea.

When I finished, Gayle waggled her eyebrows up and down. "It has a certain element of risk," she said in her finest Sherlockian tones. "You wouldn't actually attempt it, would you?"

"Wanna bet?"

That evening, by the light of a full moon, Guppy came to our campfire and told an Indian legend about how the constellations were made by a large bird pecking holes in the curtain of the sky with its beak. After Guppy left, some of the girls made up ghost stories. Sandra told one about a girl who died from being bitten by rabid bats, and then returned as a vampire who haunted the woods during the full moon. At the end of the story Sandra pounced on Kelly MacConnell, who was sitting next to her, shouting, "Bat fangs gotcha!" Kelly about jumped out of her skin!

At last it came time to head back to our cabin. As we changed into our pajamas, Shorty and Mrs. Williamson came to tell us good night. I noticed Mrs. Williamson looking with concern at the rafters— probably checking for bats!

"Get a good rest, girls," said Mrs. Williamson.

"Sleep tight," said Shorty.

"Good night, Shorty," we all said. "Good night, Mrs. Williamson."

"Cricket," said Mrs. Williamson. "Remember?"

But somehow none of us could.

As soon as the moms' door was closed, Gayle and I went to work. We whispered to everyone to meet in the corner of the cabin farthest from the moms' room. The full moon meant that we didn't need to arouse suspicion by using our flashlights.

We formed a circle, most of us propping ourselves up on our stomachs with pillows.

Gayle, once my partner in investigation, now my partner in intrigue, whispered, "Anyone ever heard of a 'white nose'?"

No one had.

"It's a trick my cousin Lee Ann played on her counselor at camp last summer," said Gayle. "When her counselor was asleep, Lee Ann snuck into her room and squeezed some toothpaste into the palm of one of her hands. Then she tickled her nose with a feather, and when her counselor put her hand up to scratch her nose she got a 'white nose' full of toothpaste!"

We muffled our giggles in our pillows.

"We could do that!" whispered Sandra. "My mom's a good sport. She'd think it was funny."

"You'd do it?" Gayle acted shocked. "To your own mom?"

Sandra thought for a minute. "It would be better if somebody else did it. I have to live with her."

Sandra turned to me. "You could do it, Lila."

"Me?"

"Yeah," said Sandra. "You're always doing crazy things."

"We could make it a bet," offered Gayle.

"Lila's probably had enough bets for one day," announced Rita. "By the way, where's the dollar you owe me from the last bet?"

"Here it is." I tossed my crumpled dollar across the circle. Rita grabbed it and slipped it smugly into her pajama top, as if she had something that would hold it there!

"So," Gayle went on, "who wants to make it a bet? A one dollar bet."

"You mean bet with our candy money?" asked Kelly MacConnell. "Are you serious?"

"This is going to be better than candy," said Gayle.

Rita nearly shouted, "I can't believe my ears! Gayle Deckert saying something could be better than candy!"

"Shhhhh!" Sandra threw a pillow at Rita. "Quiet."

Rita fumbled in her pajama top for the dollar and flung it on the floor in front of her.

"I'm in," she said.

"Hey," I protested. "I haven't said I'd do this."

"Come on," urged several of the girls. "It'd be great!"

Then, one by one, all the girls tiptoed to their bunks and got their dollars. Thirteen dollars ended up in a pile in the middle of our circle. Gayle scooped them up. "I'll hold the money while the bet's on."

I shook my head. "I don't know. . . . What happens if I chicken out?"

"We get our money back," said Sandra. "And you owe us each a dollar."

Owing thirteen more dollars was not what I had in mind. There was no way I could chicken out.

"And if I get caught?"

Sandra, Rita, and Barbara went into a huddle.

"You can keep half the money," said Sandra at last.

Half the money was $6.50. Better than nothing. So far my Great Idea was working like a charm.

"I have one condition," said Rita. "Mrs. Williamson gets the nose job or there's no bet."

"Wait a minute!" I protested. "I don't want to end up back in the Camp Director's office. Shorty'd understand it was just a joke, but Mrs. Williamson . . ." My voice trailed off as we all looked at Lynn to see what she'd say.

"My mom's not a very good sport," Lynn said in her soft voice, "but if you're brave enough to try it, go ahead."

This wasn't part of my Great Idea at all. But what choice did I have?

"Okay, okay," I said, as if giving in to popular demand, "I'll give it a try."

All we had to do now was think of an activity to keep us awake until the moms were sound asleep.

Rita suggested that we go around the circle and tell who we liked as a boyfriend. Six of us said Eddie English!

After that I got up and put my ear to the moms' door. I heard gentle, regular breathing.

"They're asleep." I went to my bedside table to collect my tube of toothpaste and a bluejay's feather I'd found on the nature trail.

"Go to it, klutz-o," said Rita. "Try not to break any windows while you're at it."

For some odd reason it hadn't occurred to me until this minute that I'd just invented an opportunity to klutz myself into some big trouble. I'd been so excited about my Great Idea for making ten dollars that I'd forgotten all about my doubtful abilities as a sneak.

Thirteen girls lay down on the floor around the moms' room so they could peek under the partition.

I was as ready as I'd ever be. I took a deep breath and tiptoed to the door. Silently I lifted the metal latch and opened the door a crack. I stood still. No change in the breathing. By the light of the moon I identified the lump in the sleeping bag nearest the door as Mrs. Williamson. She was sleeping on her back, with one hand open and stretched slightly off the bed. It seemed too good to be true! Slowly, keeping low, I crept toward her. When I was about two feet away, Mrs. Williamson gave a short snore, tucked her arms in closer to her chin, and rolled over onto her side. Her hand was slightly closed now, into

a sort of cone shape. Ever so slowly, I squeezed tooth-paste into that cone, filling it from bottom to brim, just like the soft ice cream machine at the Dairy Queen. I even put a little peak on top!

Now came the hard part. As quietly as I could, I crawled to the head of Mrs. Williamson's bed and began to slip feet first underneath it. But I hadn't counted on Mrs. Williamson's suitcase being under her bed, and I hadn't counted on her hiking boots being on top of her suitcase. As I slid beneath the bed I pushed the suitcase with my feet, and the heavy, metal spiked boots fell with a crash that sounded to me like a dozen bowling balls dropping. I froze. I waited. Shorty turned over in her sleep. Mrs. Williamson was still. These were some sound sleepers!

I pulled myself up on the metal bar that was the head of the bed, reached out my arm, and tickled Mrs. Williamson's nose, then ducked down again, out of sight. Mrs. Williamson gave no sign of noticing. I stuck out my arm and tickled a second time. Now she rolled over onto her back again. Once more I stuck out that feather and rubbed it back and forth on her face. Mrs. Williamson wrinkled up her nose, as though she was going to sneeze. Then she took her hand, overflowing with white toothpaste, and wiped it right across her nose and onto her cheek. That was the last I saw, because I slithered down beneath the bed. All around me on the other side of the partition, I could see dim shapes of heads. I hugged close to the wall and listened.

"Mmmmp!" Lips smacked above me. "Mmmaap!"

"Victoria?" It was Shorty's voice. "What is it?"

"Why . . . I'm not sure. I . . . I . . . Oh! Eeeeeeeee!" she shrieked at last. "There's something on me! On my face! Something slimy! Ohhh, it's a leech! I can't get it off!"

With that Shorty jumped out of bed, grabbed her flashlight, and aimed it in Mrs. Williamson's direction. I could see her startled face in the reflected light. She hurried to Mrs. Williamson's side, closely examining her face. Then she let out a single burst of surprise.

"Victoria!" she exclaimed, plainly relieved. "It's not a leech. It's . . . it's . . . I don't know what it is. It's just some white goo." Shorty laughed warmly. "It looks as if you've run smack into a cream puff!"

Stifled giggles rose from the outer room.

"Pfffft," spat Mrs. Williamson. "Oh, honestly. This is too disgusting." I heard tissues being plucked from a box. Then I saw Mrs. Williamson take Shorty's flashlight and aim it at the rafters. Did she think she'd find a bat directly overhead?

"Come on, Victoria," said Shorty. "I'll help you wash it off."

As Shorty went to get her robe from a hook on the back of the door, I heard the scuffle of twenty-six feet scrambling back to their bunks. I looked up to see if Shorty had heard it, too, and my heart nearly stopped. Shorty was staring right at me! I blinked, hoping that when I opened my eyes, I would find her looking somewhere else, but it didn't work. She was looking at me, and then . . . could I trust my eyes in the moonlight? Shorty winked.

Mrs. Williamson's heels were about five inches from my nose, and there they stayed while she put on her bathrobe. Shorty came over and took her arm. It seemed as if she was purposely directing Mrs. Williamson so she wouldn't look back and see me!

"I have a fresh face cloth, Victoria," Shorty said, steering Mrs. Williamson out the door.

"It's on my hand, too," Mrs. Williamson was complaining. "I just don't see how this could have happened."

As their feet disappeared around the corner, I did a silent roll out from under the bed, untangled my ankles from the laces of those two-ton hiking boots, and raced to my bunk.

I lay there, breathing hard. Everyone pretended to be asleep.

After what seemed like a long time, we saw the flashlight beam guiding Shorty and Mrs. Williamson back from the bathroom.

Shorty spoke quietly into the dark. "Good night, girls."

A single voice rang out from the bunk above me. "Good night, Shorty! Good night, Cream Puff!"

With that, everyone burst out laughing—even me. Cream Puff! Well, this is it, I thought. We're all going to be lined up against the wall until I confess. I held my breath.

"Cream Puff, is it?" Mrs. Williamson said, over the laughter. She gave a little snort. "Now go to sleep, girls."

When I woke, it was barely light outside. No one in Bat Bungalow was up yet, but I had a feeling that I knew one person who would be. I got out of bed and slipped into my jeans, sweat shirt, and sneakers. Stepping up on the side of my bed, I reached under Gayle's pillow and took out my hard-earned roll of thirteen dollar bills. I wedged the bills into my pocket.

Quietly I let myself out the cabin door. Then I raced up the hill, smiling when I saw a thin wisp of smoke coming from the lodge chimney.

Once again I knocked on the Camp Director's door.

"Come in!" This time the booming voice sounded surprised.

"Well, you're up bright and early," Guppy said when she saw me. "Broken any more windows?"

"No," I said. "But I came to pay for the one I did break."

I counted out ten dollar bills on her desk.

"What did you do, rob a bank?"

"Nope, it's all fair and square. By the way," I asked, "what time does the Camp Canteen open?"

"Not until after dinner." Guppy looked at me closely. "But perhaps we could make an exception this morning." She led the way to a small door on the other side of the lodge. After she unlocked it, I went in and picked out a bag of Junior Tootsie Rolls. Thirty to a bag for two dollars. I still had a dollar to spare.

I ran back to Bat Bungalow. No one was awake yet, so I tiptoed around and laid two Tootsie Rolls on everyone's night table, including Rita's, right next to their toothpaste. I had four Tootsie Rolls left over, and I knew just where they belonged. Back into the moms' room I snuck and silently laid one Tootsie Roll on Shorty's night table and three on Mrs. Williamson's. I certainly hoped that she was fond of Tootsie Rolls!

I crept back to the main room, stretched out on my bunk, and breathed a huge sigh of relief.

After a while the door to the moms' room opened and Shorty came out. "Morning, Lila. Did you sleep well?"

"Much better than I thought I might," I told her gratefully.

Shorty gave me another wink as if to seal our secret.

Mrs. Williamson marched out behind her, toothbrush in hand. "Good morning, Lila," she said.

Was what I felt like saying at this moment a Great Idea? Or was it the World's Worst Idea? I wasn't sure, but I took a chance.

"Good morning, uh . . . Cream Puff," I said.

"Cream Puff," she repeated. "I'm now Cream Puff?" She breezed past me as she headed for the bathroom. I couldn't be certain, but as she turned the corner, I thought I could see her smiling.

GOOD-BYE
TO FIFTH GRADE

Kelly MacConnell gave Roger Rupp a little tap on the shoulder and then slipped him the note.

I glanced up at Mr. Sherman. It didn't look as if he had seen the note being passed. He was walking up and down the aisles between our desks, reading out loud from *A Tale of Two Cities*. Mr. Sherman says that it's one of his all-time favorite books. He told us that, way back in the Pre-Video Age, when he was in the fifth grade, his teacher had read it to his class, and it was the most important thing that ever happened to him in elementary school. He says maybe one of us will become a fifth grade teacher some day and we'll read it to our class. One of us a teacher—that's hard to imagine!

Roger took a long time reading the note. Finally he folded it, held his arm down and dropped it right beneath his desk. Then, with the toe of his sneaker, he pushed it slowly forward until it was just under the back of Barney Barker's desk. Roger nudged Barney's arm with his ruler and when he turned around, Roger pointed the ruler down at the note. Barney put his heel on top of the note and scooted it forward, reached down and picked it up. Barney never noticed that Mr. Sherman, still reading aloud, was standing right beside him. As Barney brought the note up from the floor, Mr. Sherman held out his hand. Barney got a funny look on his face, but there was nothing he could do. He laid the note on Mr. Sherman's open palm. Mr. Sherman stuffed the note into his pocket. All this time he kept on reading. He never missed a beat.

Everybody had seen what had happened with the note. Everybody was probably worried, like I was, about Mr. Sherman's reading it. But in a way it was a relief not to have to think about the note going around the room. Now we could just listen and enjoy the story.

Mr. Sherman was reading the third-to-last chapter of *A Tale of Two Cities*, and this was our third-to-last day of school, so we knew we'd come out even on the last day. We all loved the story, just like Mr. Sherman did. Michael said his favorite parts were about the guillotine, which is this big wooden structure with a heavy, razor-sharp knife blade on the top. Prisoners during the French Revolution had to stick their necks into the guillotine and then—WHAP!—the blade would fall and chop off their heads.

My favorite part was the suspense of the story. In it a man named Charles Darnay, who had a wife and daughter, was about to be guillotined even though he was innocent. And the chapter we were reading now was about this friend of his, Sydney Carton, who didn't have any family and hadn't ever done anything very good in his life, but who had an amazing plan— a Great Idea if there ever was one—to save Charles. Kelly and Sandra say they like Charles Darnay the best, but Gayle and I agree that we are in love with Sydney Carton.

Sometimes Mr. Sherman would read *A Tale of Two Cities* to us after lunch for a long time, even right through math. It's a complicated story and we'd all get so involved in it that it was hard to stop. But today we stopped when the chapter ended, talked about the story for a while, and then Mr. Sherman put his tattered copy of the book down on the top of his desk.

"That's it for now," he said. "Time for you to break into your math groups."

Papers fluttered and books thudded together as we changed seats for math. I quickly grabbed my half-finished homework and walked up to Mr. Sherman's desk. Although he could be strict, he would always listen to us and consider what we had to say.

"Mr. Sherman," I said. "It's about that note."

"What's about that note?" he asked.

"I want to talk to you about it."

"Why didn't you say that in the first place?" Mr. Sherman was a great one for using language with exact meaning.

"It's not like most notes," I began. "It doesn't say 'Meet me at the drinking fountain' or anything like that."

"Hmmm," said Mr. Sherman.

"And," I went on, "I would like to ask you to throw it away without reading it."

Mr. Sherman looked me straight in the eye for a second and then he drew the note from his pocket, crumpled it into a tight ball, and tossed it into the wastebasket.

"Will that be satisfactory?" he asked.

"Thanks, Mr. Sherman," I said. "You won't regret this." And I hurried to my math group to finish up my my problems.

Math itself was usually a big problem for me. We were working on percentages and I just didn't seem to be able to figure out anything except ten percent. But today I had other problems, and they had to do with the intercepted note. What the note had said was this:

103

*Want to chip in to buy Mr. Sherman a
good-bye gift from our class? Bring
whatever you can afford to school
tomorrow. Eddie will collect money at
recess. Mrs. Fenwick will take us
shopping after school.*
> Signed,
> Eddie, Michael, Gayle & Lila

How were we going to let everyone know about our Great Idea, I wondered, now that the note was gone? I looked around the room. It was hard to remember where people sat when they were all mixed up like this for math groups. But I managed to write down the names of all the kids that I thought had gotten the note. I counted ten of them. Plus the four of us who had written the note made fourteen. Twenty-eight in our class, minus fourteen, equaled fourteen, minus two who were absent—that left twelve people to tell at recess today. Twelve people divided by the four note writers equaled three people for each of us to tell. That shouldn't be too hard, I thought.

Even though I felt like I'd already finished too much math for one day, I opened my math book and tried hard to figure out what was going on.

The second-to-last day of school was hot and sticky. It felt like August, but Mr. Sherman kept us working as if it were the middle of the year. Lucky for our plan, he stayed in at recess to grade papers, but if he had looked out his window, he would have seen some strange goings-on at the playground.

Eddie English was standing by the fence in back of the softball diamond, and most of the kids in our class were gathered around him, waiting to give him their money for the class gift. Gayle and Michael and I were sitting on the ground near Eddie, counting the change that had come in. Just as the crowd was thinning, Rita came up to Eddie.

"That's a fabulous idea you had, Eddie," she said. "Really together, to get Mr. Sherman a good-bye present."

"Yeah," said Eddie. "It was really Lila's idea, though."

I tried to hide my smile.

"Anyway," said Rita, never even looking over at me, "I wondered if I could come with you to pick out the present. I'm really a dynamite shopper."

I could tell Eddie didn't know what to say.

"I guess so." He shrugged his shoulders. "Think your mom could take an extra passenger, Lila?"

"I'm not sure there are enough seat belts," I mumbled feebly. My mom always insists that everybody buckle up in her car, and there *were* only five sets of seat belts.

"That's okay." Rita gave Eddie a big smile. "Two of us can share a belt."

Sometimes I couldn't believe the things that came out of Rita's mouth!

When the 3:30 bell rang, Michael and I walked out of the classroom together. Rita walked with us, too, telling us about the time she and her father had picked out a digital food scale for her mother at Artie's Discount Center and how that would be the perfect place to shop for Mr. Sherman's present. I saw my mom's car parked near the crosswalk. Gayle and Eddie were on Safety Patrol duty, so we knew we'd have to wait a few minutes for them. I climbed into the front seat right away, next to my mom. Somebody had to sit there, and I wasn't going to be a part of the seat belt sharing plot in the backseat. Finally Gayle and Eddie came up to the car.

"Gayle, want to share a seat belt?" Rita called.

Asking Gayle, who was far too wide to ever share a seat belt with anyone! That was low!

"No thanks," said Gayle huffily.

But before Rita could ask him, Eddie elbowed Michael and Michael said, "Eddie and I can share the middle belt. We're the skinniest."

"That's settled," said my mom. I could tell she didn't go for the seat belt sharing at all. "Where would you like to shop?"

"Artie's Discount Center," said Rita before anybody else had a chance. "They've got everything."

Since none of the rest of us had any better ideas,

we drove off toward the discount center.

What I'd been looking forward to as a great time was starting out all wrong. Gayle was miffed at Rita for the seat belt suggestion, Rita was pouting because she wasn't even sitting next to Eddie, and Eddie and Michael were squished together like Siamese twins.

"Well," said my mom to break the silence, "how much money did you collect for Mr. Sherman's gift?"

"Twenty-three dollars and eighty-five cents," said Eddie.

"You should be able to get something very nice for that amount," said my mother.

Luckily Artie's isn't very far. When we got there, my mom let us out in front of the store and went to park the car.

"Just stay together," she called after us.

The first thing you notice when you go into Artie's is that almost everything plugs in. Right away we passed the electric blankets, heating pads, humidifiers, stereos, tape recorders, blenders, and toaster ovens.

Rita stopped in front of a big blue plastic tub. It was supposed to be filled with warm water, and you could put your tired feet in it and the water would swirl around and relax them. Rita said that her mother had one of these and really used it a lot, especially in the winter. Luckily it was $35.00 and out of our price range.

I stopped at a display of Swiss Army knives. One had about two dozen attachments—tiny nail scissors, a miniature magnifying glass, a can opener, and even a little toothpick. But no one else seemed to like it much.

"You know," I said, "when I look at all these things, it makes me think that I don't know anything about Mr. Sherman. I know him as a teacher, but not outside of school—not as a person."

"I know what you mean," said Eddie. "It's sort of funny, after having him for the whole year."

"Yeah, we don't know what his house is like," said Michael, "or what he likes to do."

"Maybe we should look for something he could use in school," said Gayle.

We all liked this suggestion, but when we looked around, we didn't come up with much. There were electric pencil sharpeners, but the school had pencil sharpeners. There were lots of clocks, but the school had clocks.

My mom came in and found us.

"How are you doing?" she asked.

"Nothing yet," said Michael.

So my mom wandered around with us. I could tell she wanted to make suggestions but was trying hard to be quiet and let this be our project.

Suddenly Rita stopped in the radio section.

"This is best," she said. "Check it out."

She was pointing to a shiny white radio with red numbers on the front. It did look nice.

"My father has one of these," said Rita. "And he loves it."

I was beginning to think that Rita's house must look something like Artie's Discount Center.

"A radio might not be a bad gift," said Michael.

"This isn't just any radio," said Rita. "It's a shower radio."

"A shower radio?" asked Gayle.

"You can put it up in the bathroom," said Rita. "It's battery operated and water doesn't hurt it. My dad listens to the stock reports on his while he showers and shaves in the morning and he says he's up to the minute before he's even had breakfast."

"Mr. Sherman could listen to the news," said Eddie. "You know how he likes current events."

"If he likes *current* events," said Michael, "we should get him an *electric* radio!"

We all groaned. Sometimes Michael could make the worst jokes.

"And look," said Gayle. "It's twenty-two dollars— just about what we have."

"At that price we could even afford a battery," said Eddie.

"Wait a minute," I said. "Are you serious? Getting Mr. Sherman a *shower* radio?"

"You have a better idea?" asked Rita. "One of your so-called Great Ideas, maybe?"

"No," I said, wishing I could think of a Great Idea for helping Rita contract lockjaw. "But I'm not giving up yet. Come on, Gayle. Let's walk around and see what we can find."

We circled Artie's again. We saw electric coffee makers, electric skillets, computerized talking scales, video recorders, travel alarm clocks, orange juice squeezers, microwave ovens, and trash compactors. But nothing for Mr. Sherman.

"What's wrong with the shower radio?" asked Gayle as we walked back to find the others. "Is it just because it was Rita's idea?"

"No," I said. "I just . . . I just don't like it."

The other kids and my mom were talking to a salesman when we got back to the counter. He'd taken a shower radio out of the case for them to look at.

"Any luck?" asked Rita brightly.

"I still think the Swiss Army knife would be a good present," I said. But no one else said they did.

"Do you think Mr. Sherman would like a nice waffle iron?" asked my mother. "I noticed sort of an interesting model that makes waffles in six different shapes."

A waffle iron! I knew I should feel thankful to my mother. After all, she was just trying to think of alternatives to the shower radio. But a waffle iron!

Michael loved to tease my mom. "When Mr. Sherman opens his gift, he might say, 'How waffle!' "

We all groaned again, my mom loudest of all.

"Okay, okay," said my mom. "So much for suggestions from the over-forty set."

Then Michael turned to me. "What don't you like about the radio, Fenwick?"

It wasn't going to be easy to say what I thought. Nervously I tugged at what used to be my bangs, stuffing a clump of hair behind one ear. "I just think it's weird to get Mr. Sherman something that he'd use in the bathroom. It's too . . . I don't know. I just think it's embarrassing. Like we're all thinking about him taking a shower or something."

Rita started giggling. "Maybe you have that kind of mind, Lila."

I crossed my arms on my chest. I could feel my face getting hot. I was glad my mom had wandered away and was pretending to look at an electric exercise bicycle a few counters away so she didn't have to hear this stupid argument.

I glanced at Eddie, and he looked embarrassed. So did Michael. Gayle just looked annoyed.

"I think Lila's right," said Gayle.

"You would," said Rita.

"Oh, be quiet, Rita," said Gayle. "The radio is a little, well, personal. But the thing is, tomorrow's the last day of school. We've got to get something today. We don't have time to go to another store, so it has to be something here. And the shower radio is the best thing we've seen. So, unless we want to look around some more, maybe we should just get it."

Good old practical Gayle. But her little speech had given me an idea. I walked over to the front window of Artie's and looked across the street. There was an automotive supply shop, a pizza parlor, and a bookstore. A bookstore! Good-bye, shower radio, I thought, hello great big beautiful book! I pictured the kind of showy book people leave out on their coffee tables, one with gorgeous paintings from the Art Museum or maybe one with glossy, color photographs of African animals. Filled with the excitement of a Great Idea, I hurried back to the shower radio counter.

Eddie was tuning in to an FM station.

"I do have a better idea," I said confidently.

"What?" asked Rita. I could tell she was going to hold on to the shower radio idea like a bulldog to a bone.

"There is one thing we do know about Mr. Sherman," I said. "And that is that he loves books."

"True," said Michael. "But there aren't any books here, so what good does that do us?"

"There's a bookstore across the street," I said. "We have time to go over there and at least look for ten or fifteen minutes. If we can't find anything, then we can come back here before Artie's closes and get the radio. How's that?"

Everyone but Rita nodded.

Rita gave me a big, phony smile. "It sounds like a waste of time to me, but if it'll make you happy, Lila, we'll do it."

We told my mom the plan and crossed Hanley Road to Lackey's Book Store. It was just about the opposite of Artie's—nothing plugged in at all. There were rows and rows of all kinds of books.

"Maybe we know that Mr. Sherman likes books,"

said Eddie once we were inside, "but what kind?" It wasn't a very big store, but it seemed big at that moment.

We split up and wandered up and down the aisles. I passed cookbooks, travel books, a section on child care and one on women's studies. Nothing there. The great big colorful books of my imagination all had great big colorful prices, too, way over our $23.85. I was getting discouraged. And then, in the section labeled classics, I spotted a copy of *A Tale of Two Cities*. I slipped it out of the shelf and held it in my hand. It had a red cover and I could tell it was real leather by the smell. Inside there were black-and-white drawings every so often. And it even had a ribbon attached at the top for a bookmark.

Eddie came up behind me. "What'd you find?"

I closed the book to show him the gold letters on the front.

He smiled. "You know," he said, as if he'd just made a big discovery, "Mr. Sherman reads this to his class every year. He'd really use this."

"Just what I was thinking," I said.

While Rita was still browsing in the self-help section, Michael and Gayle came up to where we were standing. We showed them the book. I could tell from their faces that right away they knew it was perfect. We didn't even need to talk about it.

But there were two problems ahead. One was telling Rita. The other was that no price was marked on the book. It looked really expensive.

I carried the book to the counter in the front of the store.

"Excuse me," I said to the man standing behind it, "could you tell me how much this book is?"

"Nice, isn't it?" he said as he took the book from me. "I'll have to look up the price."

Rita came up to the counter as we were waiting for the price check.

"What's happening?" she asked.

"We may have found something," I said. "But we don't know how much it is."

"What is it?" was her next question, naturally.

We were all quiet. No one wanted to tell Rita.

"It's a book that we know Mr. Sherman loves. *A Tale of Two Cities*," said Michael.

We all watched Rita's face.

"You're going to get him a book you know he already has?" she asked.

"But his is paperback," I said, "and it's falling apart."

"This one's got a leather cover," said Eddie, "and a built-in bookmark."

"It'll make him think of us—of our class—when he reads it to his fifth grade next year and the next year and the next year," said Gayle.

"*If* we can afford it," added Michael.

Rita looked at us as if we had been speaking a foreign language, but, for once, she didn't say anything.

I wished the man would hurry with the price check.

At last he looked up from his notebook.

"It's priced at twenty-nine ninety-five in the leatherbound edition," he said.

My heart sank.

"But it's twenty-five percent off right now," he continued. "My calculator battery is dead, but if you'll wait a couple of minutes, I'll work out the price."

My heart popped back up again.

"Twenty-five percent," I muttered to myself, "of twenty-nine ninety-five, which is almost thirty dollars. If it were ten percent, it would be three dollars off, and twenty percent would be double that or six dollars off, and another five percent would be half of ten percent, which is half of three dollars makes a dollar fifty, plus six dollars equals seven-fifty off the original price." I was practically sweating by the time I finished my calculations.

"Or you could say thirty divided by four is seven-fifty," said Gayle.

It didn't seem fair that she could get the answer so fast. But at least we came out with the same one.

"And thirty minus seven-fifty—" I began.

"Is twenty-two fifty," finished Michael.

"We can do it," Eddie announced.

The final price with tax turned out to be $24.31. We all chipped in an extra dime to make up the difference. Even Rita.

We had the perfect gift.

Most of the last day of school was spent erasing any stray marks, as Mr. Sherman called them, from our textbooks and turning them in. We also cleaned out our desks and wiped them with damp cloths.

While we were working, a fourth grader came into our room to ask Mr. Sherman if his teacher could borrow a stapler. He looked so small and young. It seemed impossible that next year he might be sitting right where I was sitting, listening to Mr. Sherman read *A Tale of Two Cities*.

With only an hour left in the day, Mr. Sherman took out his worn copy of *A Tale of Two Cities*. He flipped around to find the last chapter and was about to begin, when the whole class, as we had planned, stood up. Kelly MacConnell, since she was our second-semester class president, gave a little speech about how much we'd liked fifth grade with him and what a great teacher he was.

Then Eddie said, "And we'll always remember the books you read to us this year, especially *A Tale of Two Cities*. And we'd like to give you this, so you'll always remember us, too." I thought it was the best speech in the world.

Eddie handed Mr. Sherman the book, wrapped in blue paper, and we all watched as he opened it. When he saw what it was, his face, well, he almost looked as if he wanted to cry!

"This is a wonderful surprise," said Mr. Sherman after a minute. "Just wonderful." He held the book to his nose and took a big whiff, just as I had done when I first picked it up in the bookstore. "Leather binding. I have a class with good taste and evidently the budget to match." Then Mr. Sherman noticed where we had all written our names in our best penmanship in the front of the book and he read each name out loud.

"I've always remembered my fifth grade teacher, Mrs. Smith," said Mr. Sherman, "and been thankful for the gift she gave me in reading this book. It was the first time I ever realized how good a book could be, and it turned me into a reader. I've tried to pass that gift on to my students each year and," he looked at the new red book in his hand, "you've given me something that shows you appreciate what I've tried to give you."

The room was very quiet. It's hard to describe how I felt as I listened to Mr. Sherman's words. I looked over at Michael. He raised one thumb as if to say, "We really did it right, Fenwick!"

Gayle turned around. Her eyes were shining.

Then a voice broke the silence. It was Rita's.

"We knew you'd like it, Mr. Sherman," she said, beaming at our teacher as if she had been personally responsible for talking the rest of us into this particular gift. "Did you see the ribbon attached to the top? It's a built-in bookmark."

There was no stopping Rita. Eddie, sitting behind me, gave me a little nudge to show that he couldn't believe it either.

Then we all leaned back in our desks—the last time we'd ever lean back in our fifth grade desks—and listened as Mr. Sherman read us the last chapter of *A Tale of Two Cities*.

About the Author

Kate McMullan was born and grew up in St. Louis, Missouri, and was graduated from the University of Tulsa in Oklahoma. In fifth grade she won a prize for guppy reproduction, an achievement that Lila Fenwick, heroine of Ms. McMullan's latest book, would applaud. Ms. McMullan is the coauthor, with Lisa Eisenberg, of a number of puzzle books, including *Fishy Riddles* (Dial), about which *School Library Journal* said, "Kids will love it." She is also the coauthor of the recently published *Buggy Riddles* (Dial). Ms. McMullan lives with her husband, artist James McMullan, and their daughter in New York City.